AR 5.6

yours truly,
LUCY B. Parker
sealed with a kiss

I really needed some advice about this crush stuff—especially the part about Beatrice thinking I was nuts for having one on her brother. Yes, my mother had been totally ignoring me ever since the move to New York, but if I told her I really needed to talk to her, she'd listen. And it wasn't like I was going to tell her what was really going on. That would've been *way* too embarrassing. Instead, I was going to do the whole "Okay, so I have this friend . . ." thing.

With the move to New York, and living with a superstar, and my mom ignoring me, and my dad about to have a baby, and having to get a new bra every six weeks because my boobs would not stop growing, and *not* having my period yet, sixth grade had already been hard enough. But now, having to find a crush that my BFF thought was acceptable? Jeez. How much could a girl take?

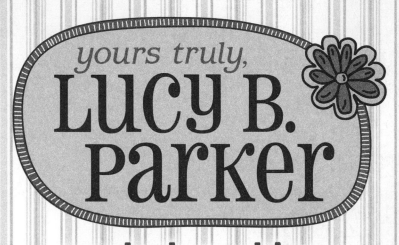

yours truly, LUCY B. parker

sealed with a kiss

ROBIN PALMER

G. P. Putnam's Sons
An Imprint of Penguin Group (USA) Inc.

G. P. PUTNAM'S SONS
A division of Penguin Young Readers Group.
Published by The Penguin Group.
Penguin Group (USA) Inc., 375 Hudson Street, New York, NY 10014, U.S.A.
Penguin Group (Canada), 90 Eglinton Avenue East, Suite 700,
Toronto, Ontario M4P 2Y3, Canada (a division of Pearson Penguin Canada Inc.).
Penguin Books Ltd, 80 Strand, London WC2R 0RL, England.
Penguin Ireland, 25 St. Stephen's Green, Dublin 2, Ireland
(a division of Penguin Books Ltd.).
Penguin Group (Australia), 250 Camberwell Road, Camberwell,
Victoria 3124, Australia (a division of Pearson Australia Group Pty Ltd).
Penguin Books India Pvt Ltd, 11 Community Centre, Panchsheel Park,
New Delhi - 110 017, India.
Penguin Group (NZ), 67 Apollo Drive, Rosedale, North Shore 0632,
New Zealand (a division of Pearson New Zealand Ltd).
Penguin Books (South Africa) (Pty) Ltd, 24 Sturdee Avenue,
Rosebank, Johannesburg 2196, South Africa.
Penguin Books Ltd, Registered Offices: 80 Strand, London WC2R 0RL,
England.

Published simultaneously in Canada.
Printed in the United States of America.

Design by Kristin Smith.
Text set in Lomba.
Library of Congress Cataloging-in-Publication Data is available upon request.

ISBN 978-0-399-25538-0
1 3 5 7 9 10 8 6 4 2

For my parents, Susann and Ken Palmer, who instilled
the belief in me that I could do and be anything
I wanted in life…as long as I got good grades
and was home by curfew.

Acknowledgments

For the incredible team at Penguin Young Readers Group—Don Weisberg, Jen Haller, Nancy Paulsen, Eileen Kreit, Scottie Bowditch, and Kristin Gilson—for their amazing support of Lucy. And, as always, immense gratitude to my goddess of an editor, Jennifer Bonnell, for knowing long before I do what it is I'm trying to say.

For Kate Lee, the world's best agent.

And for BFF Extraordinaire Amy Loubalu, who patiently reminds me during the course of every book I write that, yes, there have been other times when I've been absolutely positive that what I've written is completely unreadable but that, strangely enough, that feeling ends up passing. Even though every time she says that, I'm absolutely positive this is the time she's going to be wrong.

yours truly,

LUCY B. PARKER

sealed with a **kiss**

chapter 1

Dear Dr. Maude,

I'm sooooo sorry I haven't written in such a long time. I hope you haven't been worried or anything. Because you're so busy with the new season of *Come on, People—Get with the Program*, you probably don't have all that much time to spend thinking about twelve-and-a-half-year-old girls like me who have a lot going on in their lives and could really use help from a world-famous therapist like yourself. I WAS thinking of going down to your apartment and knocking on your door, but Pete said that wouldn't be a good idea because you're kind of a private person. Even though he knows I'm not a crazy stalker, it's still his job as the doorman at the Conran to keep regular people like me away from famous people like you. (BTW, I still can't get over the fact that we live in the same apartment building! I mean, New York City is a REALLY big place. Don't you think that's just super-weird? I do.)

Anyway, I'm fine. It's just now that I'm an official New Yorker (Rose, our housekeeper, told me that she once heard on the news that that happens after you've lived here for a month, and I've been here for one month, one week, and four days), I'm busy, like, ALL the time. Which I'm sure you understand, seeing that you haven't written me back. At all. Not even once. Even though I've written you fifteen e-mails. Sixteen, counting this one.

So much has happened this last month that I don't even know where to start, but here are the main points:

1. For the most part, things with Laurel and me are okay. I mean, after you've been an only child for twelve years and five months, adjusting to having another non-adult in the house is hard. Especially when it's actually THEIR house and NOT yours. Oh, and when you happen to be the kind of person who doesn't really mind a little—or a lot—of mess, but that other non-adult can't stand it to the point where, when she comes into your room, her right eye starts to twitch and she starts to organize YOUR things even though it's YOUR room.

2. And then there's the issue of that other non-adult being the most famous teenager in the world and the star of the hit TV show *The World According to Madison Tennyson*. Which means that while everyone in the house might treat her normally, when you're out in the world during family outings, you almost get trampled to death because suddenly she's Laurel Moses, Superstar, instead of Laurel, the Girl Whose Bedroom Is Next to Yours. But even though we don't have screaming fights like Marissa (my sort-of friend back in Northampton) and her sister do, it's still weird. Like sometimes Laurel's all friendly, and other times she acts like she wants nothing to do

10

with me and just goes into her room and shuts the door.

Mom says that's just part of being a fourteen-year-old girl, and that once I really hit puberty, I'll probably be just as moody, but I hope not. The only part of puberty I'm really interested in is the getting-your-period part, which, unfortunately, has still not happened. The boob-growing part, however, just KEEPS happening. (I've outgrown TWO bras since I got the first one last fall, if you can believe it. Totally not fair.)

3.   That's another issue—Mom. You know—that woman who I USED to see all the time? The one who'd let me watch TV with her in bed at night after the divorce with a big bowl of popcorn and wouldn't yell at me if a few pieces ended up falling under the covers, which was pretty much always because of my coordination problem? The person with whom I had Manicure Mondays, where we'd do each other's nails and she wouldn't say, "Lucy, are you sure you want to use that shade of purple, because it's awfully bright?" like some other mothers might say? The one who, when I was telling her about my day at school, would actually LISTEN instead of saying things like, "I see what you mean," at times when I hadn't SAID anything for her to know what I meant?

Yeah, her. Well, ever since we moved here she's way too busy for me. Either she's on the computer searching for places to get married, or she's at some lecture at the 92 Street Y with Alan (that's my soon-to-be stepdad), or she's driving Laurel to the studio in Queens because she

11

wants Laurel to have "some normalcy in her life instead of going places in fancy town cars with drivers." But I'll tell you what she's NOT doing—spending time with me.

4.   Which is why I'm spending most of MY time with Beatrice. Remember in my last e-mail to you I mentioned that I had finally made a friend? That girl Beatrice who also lives in our building—10D—and is in my class at the Center for Creative Learning? Well, we're now officially BFFs. We had The Talk the other day, and I feel a lot better. Even though I was pretty sure we were heading down that road, you never know for sure until you have the conversation. I know when I first met her I was worried that she was one of those overly polite kids, but she's totally not. In fact, she's probably the most New York-y New Yorker I know, the way she wears a lot of black and is sure she's always right.

5.   Alice—that girl I sat with at lunch the third day of school after spending the first two in the bathroom because the kids at the Center are a lot less friendly than they are back in Northampton—keeps asking if she can be my second BFF, but that alone should tell you why she can't. I mean, you don't ASK to be someone's BFF—it just happens. And then you have a conversation about it.

6.   Other than the two of them, and Laurel (kind of), and Pete and Rose, I haven't made any other friends yet.

And Pete and Rose don't really count because Pete is forty-nine and Rose is forty, so they're more adult-friends than friend-friends. Mom, during one of the few times she and I DID spend together recently, walking to the dentist (which totally doesn't count as quality time as far as I'm concerned), said that the reason I get along so well with adults is because I'm so precocious, which, when I looked it up, means something like mature. But during our weekly Wednesday night phone call, Dad said that I'll make more friends my own age. He wasn't willing to swear on the life of my brother-or-sister-to-be or anything, but he does think it's going to happen. Remember, my dad accidentally got his girlfriend, Sarah, pregnant? I don't know if I believe him, though. If he really thought it was going to happen, he'd swear on the baby's life, even though the baby's not coming until November.

So that's what's going on here. If you could write back and give me some advice about the Mom thing, and the how-to-make-more-friends thing, that would be great.

yours truly,
LUCY B. PARKER

P.S. If you have any suggestions as to what I might do to bring on my period, that would be great, too. I know you're not a medical doctor, but, still, I thought you might know.

If I had waited a few days to send that e-mail to Dr. Maude, I would've definitely asked her about the Crush Thing.

It was a Wednesday evening in May, about a month after I had moved to New York, and I was hanging out with Beatrice in her room. There were times I really missed my old house in Northampton, even if it was really drafty because it was so old that none of the windows shut right, but there were things about living in an apartment that were very cool. Like when your BFF lives eleven floors below you, so you just have to take an elevator there instead of riding your bike.

"So did you figure out who your local crush is yet?" Beatrice asked.

My face got all red as I shook my head. "No," I sighed. I could feel my stomach get all tight, which is what it did when I got anxious, like, say, when I heard the words "And now it's time for a mixed-fractions pop quiz." "Yesterday I thought maybe I could have one on Sam Rothenberg, but then I saw him pick his nose during science."

Beatrice shook her head. "Yeah, no crushes on nose pickers," she said. "That won't work."

I reached into my pocket for my purple pen and the Moleskine notebook I had recently started carrying around that had "Important Pieces of Advice People Have Given Me" printed on the front page. Most of the stuff in it so far had come from Pete, my doorman. Things like *Try not to make eye contact on the subway, because you never know who's going to end up being a total nutjob* and *If a tourist stops you and asks you for directions and you're not one hundred percent sure of where the place is that they're trying to go, refer them to a doorman because doormen know everything.* That one came in really handy on account of the fact that in addition to my coordination problem, my sense of direction isn't so great.

When choosing a crush, make sure they are not a nose picker, I wrote neatly. At least my penmanship was good. According to Beatrice, having a crush in sixth grade was something you just HAD to have—like a computer, or a cell phone—or else you were just plain weird. I was pretty sure that that was a New York City thing, because back in Northampton some of the more boy-crazy girls I knew had crushes (like, say, Marissa, who was always saying things like, "I think I saw my soul mate in the food court at the mall today"), but it wasn't like you were considered weird if you didn't have one.

"But I keep telling you—you need to find one," Beatrice said as she opened the e-mail folder full of e-mails she had gotten from Eli, this boy who lived in California whom she met when her family was on vacation in Mexico. He was her long-distance/vacation crush. According to Beatrice, everyone needed three crushes: a local crush, a long-distance/vacation crush, and a celebrity crush.

"Fine. I'll keep looking," I replied, shifting in my chair to try to get comfortable. I don't know why all the furniture in New York apartments had to be so hard to sit on, lots of wood and leather and sharp corners. It was the same in Alan and Laurel's apartment, too. It really hurt my butt. Our furniture back in Northampton may not have matched, on account of the fact that it came from thrift stores because Mom and Dad are "creative types" who like things with "character," but it sure was a lot more comfortable. "But I don't understand why I need *three*. It's hard enough for me to find one!"

"I'll tell you why," she said. "Because if your local one doesn't pay any attention to you, or is absent for a long period of time because he has the flu or chicken pox, then you can think about your long-distance one. And if your long-distance one stops answering your e-mails—which is what Eli is doing to me—then you can just sit there thinking about your famous one and make up stories about what it will be like when you're going to movie premieres together. Which will probably never happen. Unless you're Laurel."

I had to admit it all made sense logically. Not to mention that thinking about your crush was a much better way to spend your time than worrying about whether you were going to have a mixed-fractions pop quiz, or whether your mother was ever going to start paying attention to you again. But to be honest, if someone said to me "Okay, you have to choose: either you get your period, or you get a boyfriend," I'd choose my period.

"Hey, do you have any extra Moleskine notebooks?"

I asked. "I'll pay you back for it." Before New York, I just used regular notebooks you'd get at Target or Walmart, but now that Beatrice and I were BFFs I had gotten into the Moleskines. According to her, they were very French and not at all bourgeois, which was her favorite word. I still wasn't entirely sure what that meant. I wasn't even sure that Beatrice knew, but from what I could figure out, it was French for "totally loserish."

She handed me one. On the first page, I printed "The Official Crush Log of the Girls at the Center for Creative Learning in New York, NY."

Beatrice gasped. "You're going to start another log?"

I nodded. Back in Northampton, I had kept one called "The Official Period Log of Sixth-Grade Girls at Jefferson Middle School in Northampton, MA" because you never knew when you might need to know that information. I was the Keeper of the Periods. Everyone back there had thought it was a brilliant idea, and in New York the sixth graders seemed to like it, too— EXCEPT for Cristina Pollock, the most popular (and meanest) girl at my new school, who started calling me "Period Girl" because of it.

"*C'est brilliant!*" Beatrice gasped, which was French for "That's brilliant!" She liked to say that and *C'est stupide* a lot. "I knew I was right to choose you as a best friend. It's a good thing I happen to already know a lot of this information so I can totally help you."

"Let's start with Cristina Pollock," I said. "Who are

her crushes?" Beatrice and Cristina had been BFFs before Cristina dumped her out of nowhere. In fact, one of the reasons Beatrice and I had bonded was because we had both been friend-dumped. Not only that, but it turns out it happened just days apart. Mine was three days BEFORE sixth grade started, and hers happened three days AFTER, which we decided meant that we were totally destined to be friends.

"Well, I'm pretty sure her local crush this week is Finneas Larkin," she said. "At least that's what Alice said she heard Alexandra Brodsky and Lusia Strus say in gym the other day." Finneas was a seventh grader who, like Cristina, was also super-popular, which made them a good match. "And as for long distance, there was some boy from Connecticut she met when her family went to St. Barts for winter break that I heard she was e-mailing with. But I know for sure that her celebrity crush is Connor Forrester."

"Connor Forrester?! I know he's your celebrity crush, too, but I have to say I think he's totally gross," I said. *Teen People* may have just named him one of the Most Beautiful Teens in the world, along with his BFF Austin Mackenzie (Laurel's celebrity crush), but as far as I was concerned, any cuteness he had was completely erased by the fact that he once ate a worm on camera. According to the gossip blogs, because he was all into being as real as possible in his acting, it was a *real* worm, not a gummi one.

Before I could ask Beatrice if she thought that Cristina had kissed a boy yet, Beatrice's mother Marsha stuck her head in the door. (I'm sorry—while I was willing to put a little effort into finding a crush, I could not promise that I'd be willing to then kiss the crush. Especially after hearing that when Beatrice kissed Eli that one time his braces got caught on her bottom lip and it started *bleeding*.) Like Beatrice, her mom had a short black bob and was usually dressed all in black. Except for the rims of her glasses—they were bright red. "The Korean food is here, girls," she announced.

Like Mom, Marsha was a writer, but she wrote plays. Unlike Mom, she finished the stuff she wrote and, according to Beatrice, was pretty famous in New York. Which is why she and Nicole, Beatrice's other mother, were always going out to dinner parties. Which meant Beatrice and her brother, Blair, got to eat a lot of takeout. I, however, had to suffer through Mom's attempts to cook all the recipes in some woman named Julia Child's cookbook after Mom saw a movie about another woman who did that.

"Now, Beatrice," she said, pronouncing it *Bee-a-treech-ay*, which, according to Beatrice, was the correct Italian way to say it, even though she was Jewish and not Italian. "Blair's in charge tonight while we're out, so I want you to listen to him."

Apparently this Bee-a-treech-ay person was a character in a famous Italian poem. Like wearing a lot of black, naming your kids after famous characters in literature was also a very New York thing to do. (There were two Holdens in our class—named after this kid Holden Caulfield from a famous book called *The Catcher in the Rye*.) According to Mom, it was a very pretentious thing to do. At least that's what it sounded like she said when I was overlistening to her on the phone with her BFF Deanna a few weeks earlier. Mom says that my eavesdropping is a horrible habit. I say it's not eavesdropping. It's overlistening. There's a difference. And it's not like I can help it if I have excellent hearing. Plus, most parents would be thrilled that their child was paying attention to what they were saying, even if what was being said was technically not supposed to be heard.

Beatrice rolled her eyes. "Why can't *I* be in charge some of the time?"

"Because he's older," her mom said.

"Only by nine months!" Beatrice cried. "Plus, everyone knows that girls are more mature than boys." I hadn't met Blair yet, but from everything Beatrice had told me, he sounded just awful. She said he picked his toenails on the couch when they were watching TV, and his room smelled like someone had hidden open milk cartons under dirty socks. The reason they were so close in age was because Nicole had given birth to Blair, and Marsha had given birth to Beatrice. They were technically half brother and sister because Nicole and Marsha's gay friend Bruce was their dad.

Just then a boy with light brown hair and

black-rimmed glasses wearing a faded black T-shirt with a picture of Albert Einstein sticking out his tongue popped his head into the doorframe. "Does that mean that if I tell her to clean my room, she has to do it?" he asked.

Blair pretty much looked exactly like Beatrice had described him: a little tubby, kind of a big nose, a few stains on his T-shirt. To some girls—okay, probably most girls—he wouldn't have been considered all that cute. In fact, he probably would've been considered sort of gross. And yet...there was something about him. Maybe it was because he wasn't *so* cute that you could imagine a ton of girls liking him, therefore giving you lots of competition; and yet, on the other hand, he wasn't *so* ugly that the only way you'd understand someone being interested in him was if that person was legally blind. Or perhaps it was because, as I watched him chug orange juice straight from the carton, instead of getting grossed out like I usually did when someone did that, it didn't bother me. As I listened to the *glunk-glunk-glunk* sound he made (also something that I normally would find disgusting, but this time did not), I started to think that maybe Blair Lerner-Moskovitz could be my local crush. At least until someone better came along.

"I wouldn't go in your room for a million dollars," Beatrice said. "It's so disgusting there are probably rats living in there." Uh-oh. I wasn't sure I could have a crush on someone who was really dirty. I mean, I was unorganized, and messy in a not-really-seeing-a-point-to-putting-your-clothes-away-in-drawers-if-you-were-just-going-to-take-them-out-eventually-and-wear-them-again way, but I wasn't *dirty*.

"Shut up, Dogbreath," he replied. "I'll have you know that they did this study, and it turns out that almost every genius in history had a messy room. It's part of being a creative person." Huh. I liked the way he put that. I could definitely have a crush on someone who made messiness seem like a good thing. Not to mention that my crush had to be smart, and if he read studies about geniuses, he was definitely on the smart side. He pointed at me. "So are you Laurel Moses's stepsister?" he demanded.

I sighed. I might as well have just officially changed my name from Lucy Beth Parker to Lucy Beth Parker, Laurel Moses's Stepsister-to-Be, because that's how everyone in the world referred to me. Even Mr. Kim at the deli, and he barely spoke English. It had gotten so annoying at school that I was seriously considering getting little business cards made up that said "For information about what Laurel Moses is like, please visit her website and STOP ASKING ME."

"Yeah," I replied. "Well, I mean, not yet, but I will be. After my mom marries her dad. But according to my mom, there's no hurry," I babbled. "Especially since they can't seem to decide on a place to get married, because my mom wants to do it somewhere nature-like and Alan—Laurel's father—is afraid of bugs."

Huh. I was oversharing. Was that a sign of a crush? Then again, I had overshared to the pizza delivery guy the week before, when, as I was paying him, I noticed that you could totally see the box of Stayfree maxipads peeking out of the Duane Reade bag next to the door. And because I didn't want him to think they were mine, I said, "Oh—by the way, in case you think those maxipads are mine, they're not. They're for Aunt Flo." Which was actually a really clever thing to say, because just the week before I had learned that Aunt Flo was a synonym for getting your period. And I definitely did *not* have a crush on the pizza guy.

"So, yes, she will be my stepsister … eventually … I just don't know … when," I trailed off. I bit the inside of my cheek to shut myself up. "Ow!" I cried out.

He gave a very loud, very long burp. Could I have a crush on a guy who burped like that? I guess burping wasn't that bad. As long as he didn't do *really* disgusting things like fart "Oh! Susannah" with his armpit. That's the kind of thing where I'd really have to do draw the line. "Well, see ya," he said, walking away.

"*Now* do you see why I hate him so much?" Beatrice asked, going back to her e-mail.

I shrugged. "He doesn't seem so bad," I said, focusing on the laces of my purple Chuck Taylors. My collection was now up to ten pairs, but I tended to wear the purple ones the most because purple is my favorite color. "Actually, I was thinking … I might have a crush on him."

She looked up from the computer screen and snorted. "I know you're always saying you'd never want to be an actress like Laurel, but that was *really* good."

"What do you mean?"

"The way you said that—it sounded like you actually meant it. I mean, only a total *loser* would have a crush on my brother. Could you imagine? The idea of that … *c'est fou!*" *C'est fou* was French for "that's crazy."

As Beatrice went back to analyzing whether the "Talk to you soon" in Eli's latest e-mail meant that he would call her, or she should call him, or they'd iChat at some point, I stood up. "I should get going," I said. I really needed some advice about this crush stuff—especially the part about Beatrice thinking I was nuts for having one on her brother. My mother had been totally ignoring me ever since the move to New York, but if I told her I really needed to talk to her, she'd listen. And it wasn't like I was going to tell her what was really going on. That would've been *way* too embarrassing. Instead, I was going to do the whole "Okay, so I have this friend …" thing.

With the move to New York, and living with a superstar, and my mom ignoring me, and my dad about to have a baby, and having to get a new bra every six weeks because my boobs would not stop growing, and *not* having my period yet, sixth grade had already been hard enough. But now, having to find a crush that my BFF thought was acceptable? Jeez. How much could a girl take? I thought as I rode up in the elevator.

Unfortunately, when I got back to my apartment, Mom was drinking tea at the kitchen table with venus, her new friend from 2F who was really weird. Not only did she not capitalize the "v" of her name, but she didn't use capitals ever, not even in any of the seven books of poetry she had written ("I'm all about trying to express the idea that we are all equal, so why would I make any one letter more important than another?" she explained when I asked her why).

According to Mom, they were the same age (forty-seven), but venus looked way older, while Mom looked way younger. I think it was because Mom wore regular clothes like jeans and T-shirts with her brown shoulder-length hair either hanging down or in a little ponytail, whereas venus wore these bizarre flowy nightgown-looking things with her curly red hair up in a huge bun with chopstick things hanging out of it. According to Mom, she was "flamboyant, but harmless." At least that's what she had said to Alan a few weeks before as I was overlistening from the doorway of my room.

"Hi, honey!" Mom said as I walked in.

"Hi," I said.

"Hello, Lucy," venus said in such a soft voice I could barely hear her. That was the way she talked all the time. One time I made the mistake of asking her if she had laryngitis, and she said, "Why should I yell to be heard in this world? I have trust in the universe that those who are supposed to hear me will hear me."

"Why don't you come sit with us for a while? It'll be some nice quality time," Mom said.

I didn't want quality time with my mother and her nightgown-wearing, capital-hating friend—I wanted quality time with my mom *alone*. "Um, actually . . . I'm going to go . . . double-check my mixed-fractions homework," I lied. "But after you guys are done, there's something I'd like to talk to you about."

"Honey, is everything all right?" Mom said.

"Yeah, everything's fine." Actually, it wasn't. During the elevator ride up, I had decided that I was going to keep Blair as my local crush, even if Beatrice thought I was crazy, which meant I was either going to have to (a) convince her that she was wrong or (b) lie to her, neither of which I was too psyched about doing.

Mom gasped. "Oh my God—did you get your period?!" She turned to venus. "She's just dying to get her period."

"Mom!" I yelled. I could not believe how embarrassing she was.

"Don't you remember being her age and feeling that way?" she continued, to venus, completely ignoring me. "Is that not the cutest?"

"Mom! Enough!" I yelled louder. venus flinched. "I didn't get my period, okay?" If she told venus about the fact that I used my allowance to buy maxi- and minipads so that when I did get it, I'd be prepared, I was seriously going to move back to Northampton.

Just then Alan walked in. Of course he did. Because I couldn't have one of those lives where embarrassing things happened once in a while. I had to have one of those lives where embarrassing things happened EVERY DAY. "You got your period?" he asked nervously. "Already? Isn't that on the young side? You're not even thirteen yet. That's when Laurel got hers." I couldn't believe it. Not only were they embarrassing me—they were embarrassing Laurel, who wasn't even there to defend herself!

"I did not get my period, okay?" I said. "Now I'm going to my room."

While I waited for Mom to come see me, I took out my metallic Magic Markers to make the title page of the new crush log fancy. I even went into Laurel's bathroom and borrowed one of her bajillion lipsticks (makeup companies were always sending her free stuff because she was a star) so I could make some smooch marks on it. After what seemed like forever, I heard venus leave and hid the log in my nightstand drawer so Mom wouldn't see it when she came in. After what had just happened, there was no way I was letting her know about that. With my luck, she'd announce it in her Pilates class to everyone on the Upper West Side.

Finally, Mom popped her head in the door. "Good

night, honey." She yawned. "I'm exhausted. I'll see you in the morning, okay?"

I couldn't believe she was ignoring me again! "Don't you remember I told you there was something I wanted to talk to you about?"

"Right! Yes! I'm so sorry, sweetie." She came in and flopped down on my bed. "What is it?"

She expected me to tell her after *that*? "Just forget it," I snapped.

"Lucy, I said I was sorry. My brain is just fried today. So tell me what's going on."

"Nothing. Forget it. I'll just figure it out myself. It's no big deal," I replied. I gave the biggest yawn I could. "I'm really tired, too, all of a sudden." I got off the bed and yanked her up and shoved her toward the door. "Good night. See you in the morning," I said, pushing her out and closing the door behind me.

So much for thinking I could actually depend on my *mother* to help me out.

chapter 2

Dear Dr. Maude,

I know I just wrote to you the other day, but the reason I'm writing again is because things have gotten a lot worse. Remember I told you that my mom is kind of ignoring me? Well, you can take out the "kind of" part. Now she's ignoring me BIG TIME. Like the other night, I told her I needed to talk to her about something, and then, when she came in to say good night to me, she had completely forgotten.

So that's one of the things I need some advice about. The other is the issue of crushes. According to Beatrice, I need to get a crush because if I don't have one then people might think I'm weird. In fact, that's one of the reasons why my ex-BFFs Rachel and Missy dumped me. You're actually supposed to have three crushes—a local one, a long-distance/vacation one, and a celebrity one—but honestly I'd be happy with just one. And I found one, I think: Blair Lerner-Moskovitz, Beatrice's brother. But here's my problem: I haven't told Beatrice, even though we're BFFs and that's exactly the kind of stuff you discuss with a BFF. I tried to tell her, but she thought I was kidding because she thinks the idea that anyone would like her brother is crazy.

Okay, maybe he's not Connor Forrester kind of cute. (You know who he is, right? That fourteen-year-old actor who played the brother in that movie *And Monkey Makes Four* about the family that adopts the chimp?) But he's not AWFUL-looking. And he's creative. And he seems smart, which is a very important quality for a person you're crushing on to have. Obviously, I'll have to get to know him a little better, but as I looked around my classroom today, there aren't a lot of good crush candidates to choose from. Either they pick their nose (Sam Rothenberg) or they rock back and forth in their chair a lot (Charlie Bivins) or they compare everything to a video game (Theo Morgan). And the semi-decent ones are already taken by my friends: Max Rummel (Alice) and Chris Linn (Beatrice).

I'm not sure what to do. I don't want my BFF to think I have horrible taste in boys, but it feels weird to be hiding this from her. This boy stuff is all totally new to me. I'm going to ask Laurel for some advice, too, but it's not like she has all that much experience with regular-kid stuff other than when she plays one on her TV show.

yours truly,
Lucy B. Parker

P.S. Please—if you see BLM in the elevator, DO NOT—I repeat—DO NOT tell him I have a crush on him. Thank you.

P.P.S. BLM = Blair Lerner-Moskovitz

When Alan had first brought up the whole IBS idea, I thought it was pretty dumb, but I was glad for mine and Laurel's on Sunday, because it gave me the chance to talk to her about Blair. When Mom and I moved in, Alan insisted we start having official Parker-Moses Family Meetings on a weekly basis. And during one of our first official Parker-Moses Family Meetings, the first thing on the typed agenda (like Laurel, Alan was super-organized) was Individual Bonding Sessions. Alan said that in order for us to be a happy blended family (instead of the kind of blended family like Marissa's, where there were lots of slamming doors and everyone had to go to therapy), we would all have Individual Bonding Sessions, or IBS, with the other people in the family. ("IBS? Isn't that what Grandma Maureen has where her stomach is all screwed up and she goes to the bathroom a lot?" I had asked. Mom said that that IBS stood for irritable bowel syndrome.)

Mom and Laurel were both nature lovers (can you say b-o-r-i-n-g?), so their IBS was usually a walk through Riverside or Fort Tryon Park. For Alan and me, our IBS was usually spent at the Apple Store because (a) even though he was a guy and should have been good with computers, he was always managing to do something to his MacBook and iPhone that the people at the Genius Bar had to fix and (b) I desperately wanted an iTouch and an IBS gave me the opportunity to tell him all the reasons why it was important that I get one ("Because it's so easy to read, I'll save you and Mom a lot of money on glasses because I won't be squinting to read the screen!").

The whole IBS thing was one of the reasons I was mad at Mom. Because instead of our IBS being spent doing fun things, like, say, shopping, or looking at the cats in Petco that needed to be adopted, we went to places like the dentist. Or the doctor. Or—and this was the worst—Orchard Corset Center on the Lower East Side to buy bras. Bra shopping is horrible enough, but Orchard Corset was even worse than Barbara's Bra World back in Massachusetts. There wasn't even a real fitting room there. You just went to the back of the store and stood behind a sheet, and the ancient-looking woman yelled at you to stop squirming and watched you try on the bras. As far as I was concerned, that was torture, not quality time.

Laurel and I usually spent our IBS time shopping. One of the rules of IBS was that you had to switch off who got to choose, so we only had to go to boring places like the Container Store or Jack's 99 Cent Store when it was Laurel's turn. It was pretty weird that a huge star who was so rich she probably could've afforded to wear a brand-new outfit (including shoes) every day would want to go to places like that, but she loved them. I guess part of it was because she didn't need to go shopping for clothes, because she had Zoë, her stylist, who shopped for her and brought stuff over for her to choose from, and part of it was because organizing was Laurel's favorite hobby.

When it was my turn, I chose Urban Outfitters (my new favorite store, next to H&M, because there weren't any Targets in Manhattan) or the secondhand thrift stores down in Chelsea or the West Village, because they had a wide selection of hats. Right before school started, in the hopes of having a brand-new look for sixth grade, I had put Mom's straightening iron on one of my wavy brown pigtails and kept it there for a half hour, which, as it turned out, is not a good idea. Unless you want to burn off your hair and then get it cut so short that you look like a giant egghead with ears and have to wear hats everywhere. Eventually, Laurel's hairstylist, Roger, fixed it for me, but it was really embarrassing. Even though my hair had grown a lot since the Straightening Iron Incident, on my bad hair days I still liked to wear hats.

At first the thrift stores had really freaked Laurel out, on account of her germ phobia. But once Annie Lee, the woman who owned the dry cleaner around the corner from our apartment, convinced her that any sort of grossness came off when you dry-cleaned the stuff, she relaxed. In fact, she started to like shopping there because she could get a lot of great weird things to wear as disguises so she wasn't completely mobbed when we went to the Container Store and Jack's.

Even though I thought Alan was crazy at first, I had to admit that the IBS thing kind of worked, because the first time Laurel tried on a hat at Housing Works Thrift Store on Seventeenth Street and didn't completely freak out, it really *was* a bonding moment for us. Especially after the Hat Incident. Back on the very first day we had met back in Northampton, when the director of Laurel's movie took my hat off my head and put it on hers, she totally *did* freak out and accused me of having lice, which is a pretty horrible thing to say to a person. If someone embarrasses you that badly, it totally makes sense that you'd be more than a little upset if (a) your mother then starts tutoring the person who embarrassed you and (b) then starts dating that person's father.

It happened to be my turn to choose the IBS location, and so Laurel and I were at Andy's Chee-Pees over on Eighth Street. Now that I had a crush on Blair, I decided I needed some new outfits in case I ended up running into him on a regular basis. I picked up a cardigan with what I hoped was a fake fur collar off the rack, then put it back when I realized that unfortunately it was real. I looked over at where Laurel was going through the jewelry. She was almost unrecognizable in the overalls/baseball cap/cat-eye glasses we had gotten her at a thrift store on Twenty-third Street, to the point where, when we were on the subway, I heard one girl whisper to her friend, "That girl looks like a really ugly version of Laurel Moses."

Could I trust Laurel with my secret about Blair? Because she spent most every day on the set of her TV show (when she did go to school, it was one that was full of other kids who were actors or dancers or singers), it wasn't like she had a million friends she would tell. In fact, it was really sad, but her three BFFs were Jaycee, her personal assistant; Maya, her makeup woman; and Roger, who did her hair. And Maya and Roger were really old, like in their thirties. But what if we got in a huge fight and she decided to announce it on her website? I did NOT need kids in Japan and Turkey knowing that I had a crush on Blair Lerner-Moskovitz.

Laurel had been on the quiet side all morning, which could either mean (a) she was tired or (b) her hormones were acting up and she was going to be really moody. As I had gotten to know her better these last few weeks, it had become easier to figure her out. For instance, what seemed like stuck-up-ness on account of the fact that she was famous was just shyness. We actually had a bunch of stuff in common, like a tendency to break out on our foreheads a lot and being friend-dumped. In her case, the dumping was by this girl Sequoia, who was also famous and plays her BFF on the show. But it wasn't like it was all smooth sailing. In fact, when Mom and Alan had announced that Things Had Gotten Really Serious and they wanted the four of us to move in together, Laurel started being a total jerk.

If anyone had the right to be a jerk, it was me. *I* was the one who was getting the bum deal. *I* was the one who had to leave the town where I had lived my entire life and move to New York City, which, even though most of the streets are numbered, is still an easy place to get lost. *I* was the one who had to go to a new school where the kids were so unfriendly that I spent the first two lunches in the bathroom. *I* was the one who had to leave my dad and our Wednesday night Monopoly games and Friday night pizza dinners. Even though with the Creature coming (because Dad and Sarah had decided to not find out whether it was a boy or girl, I was forced to call it that), I was feeling a little left out anyway, and would probably be totally ignored once it was born.

That being said, New York wasn't *that* bad. In fact, there were a bunch of very cool things about it, like Pete, my doorman. And the quality of cupcakes (Billy's Bakery on Ninth Avenue was my favorite). And when Laurel wasn't being all moody, she was fun to hang out with. It was kind of nice having an older almost-sister to ask about things you didn't necessarily want to talk to a parent about. Like, say, crushes.

I walked over to her. "Hey, Laurel?"

"Yeah?" she said, putting a turquoise bead necklace around my neck and then adding a coral one. I wouldn't have thought to put them together, but the combination totally worked. I liked to think that I had pretty good fashion sense. My number one rule was "The more color the better," and I believed in it so much, I even added it to my advice notebook, even though, technically, the notebook was for advice from other people. But when it came to accessorizing, Laurel was amazing. And not only very generous about giving me tips but also about actually buying me accessories. The week before she had bought me this really cool purple silk flower barrette that I had worn every day since then.

"Do you know about this three-crush thing?" I asked.

"You mean local, long distance, and celebrity?" she asked, grabbing a scarf off a table and making into a head-band before wrapping it around my head. She was good. It was like watching someone make balloon animals.

How did someone who was so *not* a normal kid know about this? More important, how did I not know until now? "Yeah. So, uh, I know you mentioned at one point that Austin Mackenzie was your celebrity crush, but who's your . . . long-distance crush?"

"Austin," she replied.

"Wait. You're allowed to use the same person in different categories?" I asked.

She nodded.

I took out my advice notebook and jotted down, *If you are having trouble coming up with crushes, consider using the same person in both the long-distance and celebrity categories.* It wasn't exactly helpful advice for people other than myself who had trouble coming up with crushes, but, still, it was advice.

"And who's your local crush?" I asked.

"I'm between local crushes at the moment," she said. "But when I'm shooting a movie in L.A., it's Austin."

I had had no idea she liked Austin so much! We weren't even an hour into our IBS session, and it had done its job. We had bonded more than ever. "You can use the same person in all *three* categories?!"

She nodded again.

Wow. Maybe that was the trick—to find a celebrity who lived in the same town as you but also was away a lot on location, so they could be local *and* long-distance!

"Who are yours?" she asked, moving over to the eyeglasses and trying on different pairs of empty frames.

"I'm trying to figure it out. With the celebrity one, is it allowed to be an animated character?" I asked.

"Nope. Has to be someone real."

I sighed. So much for choosing Stewie from *Family Guy*. "Okay. Well, then for my long-distance one, it's this kid Andrew Milton back in Northampton."

She looked confused. "I've never heard you mention him before."

I shrugged. "Well, yeah—that's because I don't actually *know* him all that well," I admitted. "He sat diagonally across from me in Mrs. Kline's class. But he's cute.

I mean, at least the left side of his face is, because that's mostly all I saw. And he lives out of town."

"And who's your local crush?" she asked.

I took a deep breath. "That's what I wanted to talk to you about. I think I've figured out who it is. But if I tell you, you can't tell anyone, okay?"

"Okay," she said.

"Do you swear on Miss Piggy?" I demanded. Miss Piggy was my cat from home who was huge and kind of mean. Well, mean to ME, which was completely unfair, seeing that I was the one who fed her. But Miss Piggy let Laurel pet her all the time. And Laurel didn't even LIKE pets, on account of all the hair and germs, but she'd come to love Miss Piggy so much that she didn't even freak out when Miss Piggy threw up hairballs on her comforter (which, because Miss Piggy was so lazy that all she did was lie around all day eating and grooming herself, was something she did a lot). My plan was to convince Mom and Alan to let us get a new kitten so that I could train it from day one to love me the best.

She rolled her eyes. "Yes, I swear on Miss Piggy."

At that I knew I could trust her. "It's Blair. Beatrice's brother."

"Wait a minute—Blair? I think I've seen him in the elevator with her. Does he have a bunch of pimples on his forehead?"

I nodded.

"And he's a little ... um ..."

39

"Tubby?" I suggested.

"Yeah," she agreed. "*That's* who you have a crush on?"

I nodded again, but I could feel myself starting to get nervous. Maybe telling her was a bad idea. Maybe she was going to say that because he wasn't as cute as Austin Mackenzie, I obviously had horrible taste, and that even though she had thought I was sort of cool up to this point, by telling her this secret, I obviously wasn't, and now she had no interest in being friends with me even if she had to sleep next door to me every night.

"Oh. Uh, he . . . has really pretty eyes," she finally said.

I hadn't thought about that part, but he did. They were a very pretty shade of blue. Or maybe they were green. On the other hand, they may have been hazel. I couldn't really remember. "Yeah, I guess. And he's smart, which is good. And creative. Oh, and he's in the Chess Club, and in band, because he plays the clarinet," I went on. "So he's, you know, well rounded and stuff."

"Huh. I never thought of you as the kind of girl who would like someone in the Chess Club. That's cute," she replied.

"But you can tell just by talking to him that he's definitely one of the cooler people in the Chess Club. He's not, like, *nerdy* or anything. Beatrice says their moms make him do it because it will look good when it comes time to applying to college," I explained. "But there are two things I need advice on. The first is now that I have a crush, I'm not sure what I'm supposed to, you know … *do*."

"Oh, that's easy. First you Google him a lot," she said, taking off her baseball cap and trying on a floppy sun hat. When she did that and didn't freak out because of the germ thing, my chest got all puffy with pride, like when you realize that you've managed to house-train a puppy. "That's what I do with Austin."

I walked over and grabbed a T-shirt that said DURAN DURAN off the "'80s Bands" rack, but put it back when I saw that it was so faded that my bra would totally show through if I wore it. I did NOT need people seeing my bra, especially since it just kept getting bigger. "I already did the Googling part," I replied. "But that didn't get me much." Other than a picture of Blair from his bar mitzvah in the Temple Emanu-El newsletter and a mention that he had come in third during the Upper West Side of Manhattan Chess Club for Juniors tournament the year before, it didn't get me *anything*.

"Well, then how about *67ing him? That's what Madison does when she likes someone." Madison was the character Laurel played on her show, who was boy-crazy, which meant that she spent most of every show (a) talking about the boy she had a crush on that week, (b) thinking about him, or (c) embarrassing herself in front of him.

"I don't know … I kind of think the whole *67 thing is stupid." The *67 thing was what you did to block your number so that when you called someone just to hear their voice say "Hello? Hello?" over and over, they wouldn't know it was you. Alice did it all the time to Max Rummel. But because she's the kind of person who is what my dad likes to call "not the sharpest knife in the drawer" a few times she forgot the actual *67 part so he figured out it was her when her last name came up on his phone. Plus, because of my coordination issues, I'd be afraid that I'd punch the wrong numbers and end up making a call to India or somewhere and getting yelled at when the phone bill came.

"And what's the second thing?" she asked.

"Oh. Well, see, I tried to tell Beatrice that I had decided he was my crush, but she thought I was joking."

She nodded. "Yeah, I can see that."

I sighed. "Maybe he shouldn't be my crush."

"No, no! Forget I said that last part. I'm sure he's really cool."

I searched her face to see if she meant it. She didn't *look* like she was lying, but with actresses it was hard to tell because that was their job. "Oh—I forgot to mention that when I was talking to him, I got a little nervous and started oversharing. So that's a good sign, right?" I said hopefully. "I mean, a sign that I actually do have a crush on him? Because, you know, I'm not totally sure I do, on account of the fact that I've never had one before." I wasn't really sure how a crush was supposed to feel. But what I *did* know was that it took up a lot of space in your brain as you tried to figure the whole thing out.

"Definitely!"

"Anyway, I don't know what to do because I don't want to lie to Beatrice, but I also don't want to lose her as a friend, you know?"

She nodded. "I get it. Hey, I think we should ask Pete what he thinks."

"You think?"

She shrugged. "Why not? He *is* always saying he's got a double PhD in Love and Life."

"That's true," I agreed. Pete had been married twice and engaged a bunch of times, so he had a lot of experience in the love department. Because he knew the answer to pretty much anything—from where to get the best falafel in Manhattan to how to make it so there was world peace—it was worth a shot.

"You've got a crush on *Blair*?" Pete asked later, after Laurel and I got back to the Conran when our IBS was over and settled ourselves on the couch in the lobby.

I nodded, and glanced nervously at Laurel.

"Blair, as in Blair Lerner-Moskovitz, who lives in 10D?" he asked, confused. "The one in the Chess Club?"

I nodded again, turning red. The next crush I had was *not* going to be in the Chess Club.

"Huh. Okay," he shrugged. "As Mrs. Weinberg in 5F likes to say, 'Every pot has a lid.'"

I wasn't exactly sure what that meant, but I liked the sound of it. "So what do you think I should do?" I asked.

After Pete tipped his hat to Mrs. Lamstein from 3L, he gave a heavy sigh and started stroking his chin, which is what he always did right before he gave advice. "Hmm ... let me think ... twelve years old ... you ... Blair Lerner-Moskovitz ..."

As Laurel and I looked at each other, I tried not to roll my eyes. Pete always repeated it all back to you, which, when you were desperate for advice, was very annoying.

"Okay, okay—I got it!" he said. "What you gotta do is—"

"Wait! Wait!" I cried, scrambling for my notebook and pen. "I need to write this down." Once I got it out, I looked up. "Okay—go ahead."

"What you gotta do is—"

I got ready to write.

"—just be yourself," he finished.

I flopped back on the couch and sighed. "But that's the same advice you gave me when I told you I was worried I wouldn't make any friends at school!" I flipped to the first page of the advice notebook. "See? It's right here."

"Yeah, and it worked, right?" he asked as he signed for some dry cleaning from a delivery boy and hung it in the closet. That was Mom's favorite thing about New York (well, other than Alan). You never had to worry about being home because the doorman could just sign for things.

"Well, with Beatrice it did," I said.

"And Alice," Laurel added.

Now I rolled my eyes. "Oh, come on. Alice would be friends with a chair if it let her." Because Laurel didn't have a lot of experience with the friend thing, she didn't understand that some friends were so annoying you sometimes wondered if they were worth having.

"Look, Lucy," Pete said. "I didn't go to college or nothing, but I can tell you this: if you're not yourself, it always ends up biting you in the butt. I'm a doorman—we know about these things."

But I wasn't convinced. Being yourself when you were hoping to make a friend or two to sit with at lunch was one thing, but when it came to crushes? That was *a lot* more complicated. "Okay, but there's another thing I need advice about."

"Ask away," he said.

I started at the beginning and told him about the three-crush rule, and Beatrice's reaction to my announcement about Blair.

"Oh, that's an easy one," he said when I was done.

I picked up my pen again in case the advice he gave about this part was actually useful.

"True friends never judge you for your likes or dislikes," he said. "They accept all of you."

Huh. Now *that* was advice! I liked that so much that I wrote it in the notebook in all caps. It was true—Beatrice ate sardine sandwiches every day, which not only (a) smelled but which (b) I personally thought were completely disgusting, and I still (c) sat with her at lunch and (d) wanted to be her BFF.

"Ooh—that's good," agreed Laurel. "Do you think it would be okay if I mentioned it to the head writer to see if he can use it in an episode of *Madison*? I think it could be good for one of the 'very special' ones."

"Knock yourself out," Pete replied.

Just then Laurel's phone rang. "It's Howard," she said, looking at the screen. Howard was her agent. "Omigod—I wonder if it's about the Austin Mackenzie movie!" she gasped as she ran over into the corner to take the call. The week before, Laurel had auditioned for a part starring with Austin in this big film called *Twilight Under the Dark of the Moon*, about a girl who is part-witch who falls for a boy who is part-vampire. It was kind of a Romeo and Juliet–type thing, because obviously their families weren't happy about it because of the difference in species. Laurel said the script was really good. After a minute, she hung up and shrieked and did her little happy dance (which, if the paparazzi ever got a picture of, the headline would probably say "Laurel Moses Has Epilepsy!" which is this disease where you have seizures), so I figured it was good news.

"I got the lead!" she yelled.

"That's awesome!" I yelled back. This was a huge break for her because it would show her in a different, non–America's Sweetheart light. At least that's what Alan had said to Mom a few nights before when I was overlistening.

Suddenly she stopped and turned white. "Wait a minute. Lucy, do you know what this means?"

"You get to go to L.A. and have your own trailer and eat whatever you want from the craft services truck?" I replied. According to Laurel, craft services was this place that had tons of different kinds of snacks—cookies, chips, fruit, vegetables, gum, lollipops—and you could take *as much as you wanted*. For *free*.

"No. I have to *kiss* Austin Mackenzie."

Oh no! I gasped. I had forgotten about that part. There was a lot about Laurel's life that I wouldn't have minded having (like, say, her hair). But having your first kiss on-screen for the entire world to see? With the boy you had a triple crush on?

That part, not so much.

chapter 3

Dear Dr. Maude,

I'm still getting used to my new iTouch (Alan just bought it for me! Those IBS sessions really DO work!)—whicch is why there wil probably be typose but I need to practice. I don't know whyy it's so much harder on this than on Mom's iPhone but it iss. Anway so tonight at dinner

Dear Dr. Maude,

Sorry about that—I endded up pushing Send by mistake before I was done. If you have an iPhone or an iTouch, you probably know that the buttons are REALLYY sensitive. Anyway, so what I wanted to tell you is that at dinner Alan announced that we would be having an EP-MFM (Emergency Parker-Moses Family Meeting)

Dear Dr. Maude,

Sorry again. Okay, I'm going to stop for now because this is REALLY annoyng so I'll just e-mail you later from the computer.

The last time Alan had called an EP-MFM, it was to give us a demonstration of the remote control for the new TV, so when he announced during the "Announcements" part of dinner on Wednesday night that we would be having an emergency meeting at breakfast the next day, I wasn't too concerned. I did, however, ask why, if it was an emergency, we weren't just having the meeting right then, but because Alan is really big on sticking to schedules, he said that emergency meetings should be held outside of family dinners. The whole thing was so logical that it didn't make sense to me, so I just let it go.

"Can you just give me a *hint* of what the emergency is?" I asked Mom as she helped me change the sheets before I went to sleep that night. As I was getting into bed, I had noticed a tiny red mark on the bottom one and started freaking out that I had FINALLY gotten my period the night before and hadn't even known it. (Why the blood went directly to the sheet rather than onto the pad I was wearing was a little confusing, but apparently that's what had happened.) I ran into the kitchen where Mom was reading this book called *How to Blend a Family Without Overstirring It* and dragged her into my room to see it, and we found an uncapped red pen in the bed, which (a) explained the red mark, (b) made Mom *really* mad because they were brand-new lilac sheets to match my recently painted purple walls, and (c) made her even MORE mad when we looked closer and found a bunch more red marks, which meant that the sheets were completely ruined.

"It's not really an emergency," Mom said, making what she called hospital corners with the sheets on her side. I just shoved my side of the sheet under the mattress. I was still mad at her about the other night (not to mention bummed that I hadn't gotten my period) but had asked her for help because (a) the sheets were too high up in the linen closet for me to reach and (b) she was a lot better at making beds because she had had more experience. "It's more like a . . . surprise."

"Then why did he say it was an emergency?"

"Because I told him we already had too many different kinds of meetings to keep track of," she replied. The other day when I was overlistening, I heard her tell Deanna that apparently love was blind *and* deaf, or else there was no other way to explain how she could put up with someone like Alan, who was so neurotic. *Neurotic* was a word you heard a lot in New York, and basically it meant "annoyingly crazy." According to Pete, about 99 percent of the people who lived in our building were neurotic. (Thankfully, according to him, I was part of the one percent that was not.)

I stopped stuffing the sheets under the mattress. "You're not pregnant, are you?" I asked. If Mom was pregnant, that would not be good. In fact, it would pretty much be the most awful thing that could happen in my life: because (a) I already had a brother or sister coming, and (b) Mom was so old, she probably had to go on drugs to get pregnant and would therefore end up having triplets like Mrs. Walker in 8F. If that was the case, I was definitely moving back to Northampton to live with Dad even though (c) I'd have to sleep on the sofa bed because there wouldn't be a bedroom for me, and (d) I really loved the color of my new walls. And there was no way I was spending my entire teenagehood babysitting *three* kids at once instead of just one. Especially when I probably wouldn't even get paid for it because they were related to me. I squinted at her belly. It *was* looking a little more poochy than normal.

"God, no!" she said. She patted her stomach. "This store is closed for business." She stopped with the hospital corners and squinted at me. "Lucy, are you wearing your *bra* underneath your pajama top?"

I nodded.

She squinted even more. "Is that your old bra? The one that doesn't fit you anymore?"

I nodded again.

"Why on earth would you do that?"

"Because Marissa e-mailed me last week to say she heard that your boobs grow the most at night and that if they're bound up tight, they won't grow as much. Or as fast," I replied.

She just shook her head and sighed and gave me one of her okay-that's-so-ridiculous-I'm-not-even-going-to-respond looks. Luckily, she didn't tell me to take it off.

I have to say, the next morning when I checked them out in the shower, I could have sworn they had shrunk a bit. I was so happy that for once in her life Marissa had actually been *right* about something (she sure hadn't been right when she said that putting a teaspoon of olive oil on your hair in the shower helped it grow—all it did was make mine incredibly greasy) that when the four of us sat down at the dining room table the next morning and Alan said, "Girls, we have a surprise for you," I was actually excited to hear what it was.

"We're getting a new kitten?" I asked excitedly. I glanced over at Miss Piggy. I swear she gave me a dirty look.

"Nope," Alan said.

"You're pregnant?" Laurel asked, worried.

"Why does everyone keep saying that?" Mom asked. She patted her belly. "Do I really need to start going to the gym *that* bad?" She sighed. "Anyway, the answer is no—I'm not pregnant."

"So what is it?" Laurel asked.

"Well, now that you have your dates for the movie—" Alan started to say.

"—we thought that it would be nice for Lucy to go out there for a week!" Mom finished.

I tried not to roll my eyes, but this finishing-each-other's-sentences thing that they had recently started doing was a bit nauseating. Next thing you knew they'd be wearing matching velour jogging suits like the Pearlstines in 6B.

Laurel and I looked at each other. "You mean all of us go out there?" I asked. "Like on a family vacation even though we're not officially a family yet?" Although Mom kept saying there was no rush for them to get married, I just wished they'd make it official already because this almost-my-stepfather-and-stepsister-but-not-quite-yet stuff took a long time to explain to people. In fact, in order to save time, the other day I had decided that I was just going to start calling Laurel my "frister," which was a combination of sister and friend.

"No. Just the two of you!" Alan said. "It'll be like—"

"—your first real semi-grown-up vacation!" Mom exclaimed. "Isn't that *exciting*?!"

Exciting? Um, no. It was more like my mother dumping me yet *again*. When she and Dad were married, they never went on long vacations without me. Maybe a weekend away here and there, but never an entire *week*.

"Not to mention it will be a fantastic way for the two of you girls to bond even more!" Alan added.

I looked over at Laurel. Because she was an actress, she had what Dad called a "really good poker face," which meant it was next to impossible to know what she was thinking. Unless the conversation was about Austin Mackenzie—then she got this dreamy look on her face. "But why aren't you coming?" I asked.

Mom and Alan looked at each other. "Well, you see, uh," she began nervously.

"An old college friend of mine has an apartment in Rome that he offered to let us use—" Alan went on.

"So, basically, you guys want to go away alone so you can—" I almost said "do it," which is what Marissa said was the number one reason why adults left their kids and went away, but thankfully I stopped myself.

"—have your own bonding time," Laurel finished.

"That's exactly right!" Mom said, relieved. "Laurel, I can't get over how perceptive you are!" She turned to Alan. "Has she always been this way?"

I rolled my eyes. Oh sure— let's gush all over Laurel. Go ahead and just ignore Lucy some more.

"So what do you think, Lucy? Are you excited?" Alan asked. "Your mom says you've always wanted to go to California."

Well, yeah—I did. But I wanted to go as *me*, Lucy B. Parker, with my family—not as the tagalong little frister of a ginormous star. Yes, Alan's weird IBS sessions were working somewhat. But a few hours at the movies or a clothing store was totally different than seven days alone in a hotel room with someone, no matter how big the room was (which, in Laurel's case, because she was such a big star, probably meant the size of most people's apartments). Plus, there was the whole no-adults-around thing. Right now, Laurel wasn't like Marissa's sister, where every other line out of her mouth was "Because I'm older—that's why," but what if she became that person because Mom and Alan weren't around to referee?

"When would it be?" I asked.

"Well, in looking at Laurel's shooting schedule, and the flights to Italy, if you were okay with it, we were thinking that maybe you'd miss the last week of school," Mom said.

Huh. So I'd get to start my summer vacation a week early? That part made it a little more interesting. In fact, it was pretty awesome. Usually, I looked forward to the end-of-the-year parties, but when you're still considered the New Girl, have only two real friends, and the most popular girl in school calls you "Period Girl," you don't wake up dying to go to school every day.

"Can I order room service?" I asked. Mom barely ever let me order room service because she said they charged you almost double for what you paid in their hotel restaurant.

Alan laughed. "Yes, you can order room service."

This was getting better. "And do we get to fly first class?" Whenever Laurel flew for work, it was always first class.

Alan nodded. "Yup. And you get to stay in a suite at Shutters on the Beach."

"Oh, I love Shutters!" Laurel cried. She turned to me. "It's literally on the beach. Wow—I've never actually had a *friend* with me when I was working," she said. "That would make it so much less boring . . . and less lonely." According to Laurel, when you were making a movie, most of your time was spent waiting in your trailer until it was time to go out and do your scenes over and over again before going back to your trailer again. She turned to me. "What do you think?" Laurel's poker face was gone. In fact, she looked really excited. Like as excited as she did when the Container Store had their big half-yearly sale.

When Laurel said things about being lonely, it made me feel like an awful, horrible person for having bad thoughts about her. "I think it sounds . . . great," I said. I hoped it sounded somewhat convincing, because, unlike her, I was NOT a great actress. I hadn't even been able to get a role as a munchkin in *The Wizard of Oz* in third grade, and everyone knows that's next to impossible to do.

How bad could it be? I'd miss school and get to fly first class and order room service. Plus, I had never been to the Pacific Ocean before. It was a lot better than going to the Grand Canyon in a Winnebago like Alice's family was making her do for their summer vacation.

Not only that, but it would give me time to figure out how to deal with the fact that my own mother didn't seem the least bit guilty about shipping me off for a week so she could go "do it" nonstop in a foreign country.

"I can't *believe* you get to meet Austin Mackenzie," screeched Alice for the fifth time at lunch later that day. Austin was her celebrity crush, too.

I covered my ears. I was a loud talker, but Alice was deaf in one ear, so she literally screamed half the time. Even though she couldn't help it, it was one more reason why I wasn't so hot on having her as one of my BFFs.

"I bet that means you'll meet Connor Forrester, too," said Beatrice for the sixth time. "You're so lucky you get to go to L.A.," sighed Beatrice. "That's almost as cool as going to Paris." Beatrice was going to be a famous writer when she grew up and live in Paris and have lots of boyfriends and a parrot that only spoke French. "If you want, you can use Connor as your celebrity crush the week you're there. I'll share."

"And he'd be your local one, too!" added Alice.

I cringed. "Okay, no offense, because I know he's already your celebrity crush, Beatrice, but there is no way I could ever have a crush on someone who ate a worm." A chess player was one thing, but a worm eater was a whole other.

Just then a very tall girl named Angela Springer walked up to the table. I didn't really know her, other than the fact that everyone wanted her on their team for volleyball.

"Are you that New Girl who's keeping the crush log?" she asked me.

"Omigod—Lucy, you're really getting famous!" Alice gasped.

I craned my neck to look up at Angela (boy, was she tall!) and nodded, taking the log out of my bag. I wasn't wild about the New Girl part, but it *was* nice to feel like people knew who I was.

"Okay. Here are mine. Celebrity: Shaquille O'Neal."

I started writing. I knew who he was—a famous basketball player.

"Local: Grant Heath—he goes to Dalton." Dalton was another private school in the city, on the Upper East Side.

"And long distance, Amy Doyle."

I looked up at her.

"Yeah. We went to basketball camp together last summer. She lives in Connecticut."

I shrugged and wrote it down. "Okay, you're all set," I said. "Just make sure to let me know if there are any changes so we can keep your records up to date." I counted the entries. So far there were twenty-five.

"Omigod! Cristina Pollock is walking *right toward us*!" Alice screamed.

As I looked over, I saw that sure enough, Cristina Pollock had gotten up from her seat smack in the middle of the Most Popular table in the Most Popular section of the cafeteria and was coming over to where we sat on the edge of the Non-Popular section.

"Way to take away my appetite," Beatrice grumbled.

I looked down at her sardine sandwich. As far as I was concerned, *that* was enough to take away a person's appetite. But I totally understood why she hated Cristina so much. At least in my case Rachel and Missy had called me from the mall to tell me they were dumping me—Cristina hadn't even bothered to tell Beatrice. Beatrice had to hear a group of girls talking about it in gym class.

"Hi, Lucy!" Cristina said, all friendly when she got to our table.

"Um, hi?" I said, all suspect. I was getting used to kids being nice to me because of Laurel (well, at least until they realized I wasn't going to introduce them to her—then they went back to pretty much ignoring me), but with Cristina it was different. Even though it had been over a month ago, she still hadn't gotten over the fact that I had turned down her invitation to sit with her at lunch and was being a total jerk to me. It had taken everything in me to not say "Look, I know that the only reason you asked me to sit with you is because you want to use me to try to become friends with Laurel so you can be on her show," but I didn't, because (a) then she'd know I was overlistening when she was talking to her BFF Chloe in the girls' room and I was in one of the stalls, and (b) I was afraid that she'd use her powers as the most-popular girl in sixth grade to somehow make me even more unpopular than I already was. Not like a person with the nickname Period Girl can get much more unpopular.

I tried to hide the crush log from her, but it was too late. "So I heard you have a new log," she said, pointing to it.

I nodded. I really hoped my face wasn't too red. If she gave me another nickname because of this, that would not be good. Not like anything could be as bad as Period Girl.

"Can I see it?"

"*No*," Beatrice said. "Only people who are *members* can see it."

Uh-oh. What was this whole "member" thing? We hadn't discussed this. Plus, Cristina was the first person we had put in there.

"How do you become a member?" she asked, flipping her long blonde hair. It wasn't fair that someone as mean as Cristina had such pretty hair.

"It's an invitation-only thing," Beatrice said.

"Hey, do you want to know who mine are?" Alice asked. "My celebrity one is—"

"Actually, no. No, I don't," Cristina stopped her. "Well, I'm inviting myself to be in it."

I turned it to a new page so she wouldn't see that her name was already there and got ready to write.

"So under celebrity crush, you can put . . . Connor Forrester." She smacked her forehead. "Omigod, what a coincidence—you're probably going to get to meet him, right? When you go to L.A. with Laurel for the new Austin Mackenzie movie?"

Thanks to Alice and her big mouth, everyone had heard about that—even the eighth graders. I don't know why Cristina thought she had a shot at acting, because if this whole performance was any indication of her talent, she was *really* bad.

"Maybe," I said suspiciously. I could see that she was holding something behind her back.

She held out an eight-by-ten print of her yearbook photo. "I was wondering if you could give him this when you do," she said. *Dear Connor*, it said on the back, *If you ever come to New York City, I'd be happy to be your personal tour guide. Sincerely, Cristina Pollock, 212-555-0175.*

"Okay," I said. *Not.* I'd be throwing *that* in the garbage when I bused my tray.

"Thanks," she said. "He's soooo cute. Everyone knows that I can pretty much get any boy in New York that I want, but I'd totally take myself off the market for him."

Beatrice rolled her eyes. "He's fourteen—I'm sure he's just dying to go out with a sixth grader."

She shrugged. "You never know. Some guys like

younger women. My dad's new girlfriend is fifteen years younger than him."

"Yeah, well, if he did, what makes you think that he won't take one look at Lucy and fall madly in love with *her*?" Beatrice asked.

"*What* are you talking about?" Cristina and I said at the same time. The odds of that happening were as good as my waking up the next morning to find that my old 32A bra fit.

Beatrice shrugged. "You never know."

I snorted. "Yeah, right."

"Exactly," Cristina said. It was probably the only time ever that we had agreed on something. "Well, I should get back to the popular area. I'm starting to feel a little nauseous over here." She gave me one last fake smile. "Thanks for giving him the picture."

"But you didn't tell us your other crushes!" Alice yelled after her.

As I watched Cristina walk away, I took out my advice notebook. *When trying to get boys to notice you, make sure your hips swing from side to side.* It wasn't something I wanted to do, but it seemed to really work for Cristina.

Maybe if I ever got this crush thing figured out, I'd try it. Except that knowing me and my coordination problem, I'd fall and break my ankle.

"You're not going to believe this," Laurel said as she poked her head into my bathroom as I was brushing my teeth that night.

"Mmmwwhff?" I said, which was teeth-brushing-ese for "What?"

"The movie is shooting at Olympus Studios."

At that, I almost swallowed the toothpaste in my mouth. I knew exactly where Olympus Studios was. At the beginning of every episode of Dr. Maude's show, the announcer would say, "And now, from Olympus Studios, smack in the middle of Hollywood, California, it's time for another enlightening hour of *Come On, People—Get with the Program* with relationship expert Dr. Maude!" Not only that, but I knew from that month's DrMaude.com newsletter that she was going to be spending the entire month of June out in L.A. taping her shows, which meant we'd be there AT THE EXACT SAME TIME.

"Do you think maybe I could be in the audience of Dr. Maude's show?" I gasped after I spit it out.

"I just e-mailed Alex to see what he can do," Laurel replied. Alex was Laurel's agent's assistant. Being able to boss around people in their twenties was pretty cool. The organizational stuff might drive me crazy, but Laurel was super-thoughtful. "I'm really glad you're coming," she said shyly, giving me a quick hug.

"Me, too," I said, hugging back. I wasn't lying—the more I thought about it, the more excited I got. Even before I heard about the Dr. Maude thing.

"Are you wearing a bra?" she asked.

"Yeah."

"Why?"

"So my boobs will shrink," I replied.

She sighed. "I'd do anything to have your chest."

As far as I was concerned, she could have it. Who knew what could happen, I thought as I got into bed. Maybe being together for a week without parents *would* make us a lot closer. And then, just as I was about to drift off to sleep, it hit me, and I shot up in bed. Why settle for just being in the audience of Dr. Maude's show? Why not try to get on the show as a *guest*? I found it hard to believe that anyone needed as much advice as a sixth grader. This would be awesome—I could have all my problems solved in one hour, and I'd be completely happy for the rest of my life and would never have to worry again!

chapter 4

Dear Dr. Maude,

GUESS WHAT?! Mom and Alan are sending me to L.A. with Laurel for a week to hang out with her while she shoots the new Austin Mackenzie movie! Without them, because they're totally dumping us and going to Italy for a week probably so that they can do it nonstop. As you can see, I wasn't lying about my mother totally abandoning me, so I really am going to need some advice about all that.

But that's not the reason I'm writing. (Although if you FINALLY end up writing me back, I hope it's to give me some advice about what a person should do when her own mother doesn't have any time for her.) The reason I'm writing is because it turns out you and I will be in L.A. AT THE SAME TIME. In fact, I was thinking that maybe you'd like to have me on as a guest! I don't want to put you on the spot or anything, so I'll give you some time to think about it. And if for some reason you say no, I'll be okay with that. Even though I think it would be a big mistake because you'd probably get really high ratings on account of the fact that I have a lot going on in my life that would make for very interesting television. But if you do say no, if you could at least get me a ticket to just sit in the audience, that would be great.

Thanks very much.

yours truly,
LUCY B. Parker

The next night as I was Googling "symptoms of a crush" instead of doing my mixed-fractions homework ("oversharing" didn't come up anywhere in my search), Beatrice texted me. *Want to come down and watch America's Worst Dancers with Blair and me?*

Here was my chance to spend more time with Blair and find out if what I had was a crush. And to see what color his eyes were. *Sure*, I typed back. *I'll be down in a few minutes.* Looking down at my hairy legs and cruddy shorts, I realized going up there in shorts wasn't going to win me any points with Blair if I *did* have a crush on him, so I grabbed the first thing my hand landed on in my closet, which was a denim miniskirt. After pulling on my rainbow tights and a Beatles T-shirt, and putting my purple flower in my hair, I was ready to go.

Okay, Lucy, whatever you do, be cool and DO NOT ask about Blair, I thought to myself as Beatrice let me in and we made our way to the living room. A very tall man was dancing the tango with a very short woman on TV. "So where's Blair?" I blurted out.

"In the kitchen, putting together some disgusting food combination, like usual," she replied.

I couldn't believe we had that in common—I *loved* disgusting food combinations. Like, say, egg noodles with peanut butter. That was a good sign. *Okay, Lucy, whatever you do, just keep your butt planted on this couch and DO NOT go into the kitchen. Let him come to you.* I started fake choking, sounding like Miss Piggy right before she hacked up a hairball. "Hey, is it okay if I get some water?" I gasped.

She stood up. "Sure. I'll get you—"

I popped up. "No! I know how much you love this show. You stay and watch it. Water's in the kitchen, right? Where Blair is?"

When I got there, he was standing at the counter eating from a bowl. "I can't believe there's another person in the world who puts Cinnamon Life on top of their ice cream!" I said, amazed.

"Well, *yeah*," he said with his mouth full. "The saltiness of the oats mixed with the sugariness of the ice cream is the perfect combination."

"That's what I always say!" I exclaimed. Ice cream really had a way of bringing people together. In fact, when Laurel and I ran into each other at Scoops, my favorite ice-cream place in Northampton, and I saw that we liked the same combination (peppermint stick and mint chocolate chip ice cream with hot butterscotch and hot caramel, whipped cream, and M&Ms), I realized that maybe Laurel wasn't the stuck-up superstar I thought she was. Well, that and the fact that she looked like a normal girl because she had been crying for hours because she had been friend-dumped.

"What's your name again?" he asked.

"Lucy. Lucy B. Parker. I'm Beatrice's best friend. We met once before," I said. "Before Korean food. You were wearing an Albert Einstein T-shirt and said creative people were messy." Again with the oversharing. This was not good.

"That's weird that you remembered all that," he said.

I shrugged. "I have an excellent memory. And excellent hearing." I tried to think of something else to say, but my mind was blank, so I was silent. He was, too, except for the crunching. If you really liked someone, weren't you supposed to have like nine million things to say to them and never run out of conversation? That's the way it was with Mom and Alan and Dad and Sarah. Except it was also that way with Mom and Dad now, and they've been divorced for a year and a half. Maybe I just came from a family of people who talked a lot.

Beatrice stuck her head in. "Lucy, you're missing the blind people salsaing!" she said before going back into the living room.

"Well, uh, I guess I should go," I said.

"Okay," he said, swigging from a milk carton.

"So I guess I'll see you around," I said.

I waited for him to say, "Hey, I was thinking, maybe you want to go across the street to the park and go Rollerblading sometime" or "Maybe we should exchange e-mail addresses"—anything, something that would make me think that maybe I was on the right track with this crush thing. But all he said was, "I guess." And then he burped again.

Great. I was leaving just as uncertain about this whole crush as I had been before I walked in the door. And I *still* didn't know what color his eyes were!

chapter 5

Dear Dr. Maude,

I don't have a lot of time to write because my dad and Sarah are going to be here any minute. They decided last night to come down for the weekend, and I'm really hoping that Dad's not lying when he says it's just because they miss me a lot and want to see me before I leave for L.A. instead of some OTHER reason—like, say, they're coming to tell me in person that Sarah is actually having twins or something equally horrible. Because if that's the case, I'm going to be VERY upset. There's only so much a person can handle at one time, and between Mom abandoning me and trying to figure out if what I have is actually a crush, I have a lot on my plate at the moment.

Anyway, I leave for L.A. on Friday. I'm starting to get really excited. That being said, by the time I get back Blair will be gone. Beatrice told me yesterday that they're going to their grandmother's house in the Hamptons for a week before they go to camp. So unless something happens between now and Friday, I'll have to wait ten whole weeks to see him. Which might not be such a bad thing. I mean, who knows—maybe I'll meet a better crush in the meantime. You know, one where I actually know for sure that that's what it is.

Uh-oh—Pete just called up to say Dad and Sarah are here. Wish me luck.

yours truly,
Lucy B. Parker

P.S. Not to be a pain or anything, but if you could let me know whether you want me to come on the show ASAP that would be great.

The first thing I did when I saw Dad was burst into tears. I felt really stupid, but going from being able to see your father whenever you want to once a month is a big shock to the system. I really missed him. Unlike a lot of kids I knew, whose dads were what Mom called "emotionally unavailable workaholics" (at least I *think* that's what she said about Marissa's dad, since I had been standing at the top of the stairs in our old house when she said it and that wasn't the easiest place to overlisten from), my dad was very available and very emotional. Any sort of commercial that had to do with holidays or weddings or graduations made him cry. In fact, he was so into spending quality time together that he didn't even mind doing girl stuff like going shopping. Although if it happened to be at the Holyoke Mall, he'd mutter about how chain stores like the Gap and Banana Republic were ruining the world.

"Monkey girl!" he cried as he smothered me in a huge hug. Mom called me "jelly bean," and Dad called me "monkey girl." Well, that's what they called me until I'd turned ten and told them they couldn't anymore because it was stupid. However, on special occasions, I let them do it, and seeing my dad now seemed to fit into that category.

"Hi, Dad," I said, sniffling. I could feel my head getting wet, which meant *he* was crying, too. It was great to feel loved, but I wish it could've happened on a day when I wasn't having such a good hair day. Even though my own eyes were teary, my vision wasn't so screwed up that I couldn't see Sarah as she waddled into the apartment. In fact, a person would have to be legally blind with very dark sunglasses on *not* to see her, on account of the fact that even though she was only five and a half months pregnant, she was huge.

"Sarah, what . . . *happened*?" I gasped, letting go of Dad. When I had said good-bye to her in Northampton, you could barely tell she was pregnant. Dad had called it a "food baby" because she looked like she had just eaten a huge Italian meal. But now? Not only was her belly huge, but everything else was—her boobs, her butt. Even her hands looked bigger.

She laughed. "Apparently I popped."

Popped?! It was more like she had exploded. By the time the Creature arrived, she was going to look like a float in the Macy's Thanksgiving Day Parade.

"A few weeks ago when I was in 7-Eleven picking up some green tea, I saw these things called Tastykake Butterscotch Krimpets—have you ever heard of them?" she asked.

Um, *yeah*. They were number seven on my Top Foods of All Time list.

"Anyway, I haven't been able to stop eating them since," she said.

"I finally went ahead and ordered a case of them," Dad explained.

Yeah, it showed. Seeing a pregnant woman gain weight wouldn't have been such a weird thing, but this was Sarah, a yoga teacher who thought sugar and bread were evil and pretty much ate only boring salads without any good stuff in it like mozzarella cheese or chickpeas. The idea of her stuffing her face with Tastykakes was like something you'd see in a horror movie.

It turned out it wasn't just Butterscotch Krimpets that Sarah craved. Dad and I walked our way across New York that afternoon, but Sarah *ate* her way across it. After we went to the Rubin Museum (they specialized in Buddhist art, which is why Dad wanted to check it out), we must have stopped at every pretzel cart, hot-dog cart, and Mister Softee ice-cream truck between the West Village and SoHo. Lucky for her, there was a street fair on Sullivan Street, which meant a ton of fried food. At first I tried to keep up with her, but once I started feeling nauseated, I gave up.

As she chomped away on a corn dog, she patted her stomach. "I sure hope Ziggy doesn't go into lard withdrawal after he's born."

"Who's Ziggy?" I asked.

Dad put his arm around Sarah's shoulder. Was it just my imagination, or had her arm gotten flabbier in the few hours she'd been in New York? "Ziggy . . . is going to be your *brother's* name!" he said, excitedly.

"Wait a second. You found out the Crea—I mean, the baby—is a boy?!" I cried. At least a boy was better than a girl. While the baby might replace me as Dad's favorite kid, I was still going to be his favorite *daughter*. Unless they had another baby after this one and it was a girl. Then there was going to be trouble. "What happened to being surprised?"

"Not knowing the sex made it too difficult to bond with him," Sarah said as she nibbled on a fried plantain, "so we found out the other day."

"And that's part of why we wanted to come down this weekend—to tell you in person," Dad added, "so we can all process the news together as a family."

Aha—I was right. This trip *wasn't* about his missing me. It was about the baby with the horrible name. Just like probably everything would be about the baby from now on. Was I ever going to be special to *anyone* anymore? The divorce part of my parents' divorce hadn't been the hard part—*this* part of the divorce, when they ended up meeting other people and starting new families, was the hard part. And why were my parents so big on processing and blending and sharing? Why couldn't we just be like normal families and eat dinner in front of the TV and not talk? I was getting sick and tired of my family. Maybe I could get Pete to adopt me. I'd have to learn Spanish, but that would be okay. Or Rose—it would be cool to go to Jamaica with her to visit her family. "You can't name him *Ziggy*," I said.

"Why not?" he asked.

"Because…well, because…," I sputtered. I was going to say, "Because with a dumb name like that, he's definitely going to be chosen last for kickball and kids will throw spitballs at him on the bus—"

"Ziggy was my grandfather's name," Sarah said, all misty-eyed. Oh great—she was one of those pregnant women who cried a lot. "He always used to tell me that I could be anything I wanted when I grew up."

Dad's dad used to say the same thing to him, and he had a *normal* name: William. Which wasn't bad because then you could choose from a bunch of nicknames, depending on your mood: Bill, Billy, Will, Willy. *And* you could spell them with a *y* or an *ie*.

"Ziggy was actually his nickname," Sarah went on. "His real name was Peter. But when Greta from the yoga studio did the numerology, Ziggy was a more positive name, and apparently he'll live twenty years longer than if his name is Peter or Malachi, which is the other name we were considering."

Malachi?! This poor kid had no idea what was in store for him once he was born.

Dad turned to her. "Honey, the more I think about it, I really think the bathtub option is the way to go."

"What bathtub option?" I asked.

"I'm going to deliver Ziggy in the bathtub at home!" Sarah said. "Studies show that babies born in water live a lot longer."

Oh man. He wasn't even born yet, and already his life was a mess.

If I really wanted to make sure I had good karma (it was a Buddhist thing that basically meant luck), I'd move back to Northampton to protect him, even if it meant sleeping on a sofa bed because he had taken over what should've been *my* room.

"Ziggy Elias Parker," Dad said excitedly. "Doesn't that sound like the name of someone who comes up with the cure for cancer or solves the global warming crisis?

"Actually, no," I wanted to say. But I didn't. It sounded like the name of someone who eats glue and moves his lips when he's reading. The good news was that I had four more months to try to convince them to give the baby a normal name . . . and then he would owe me for life and have to do whatever I told him to do once he was old enough to understand how I had saved him from a lifetime of misery.

Sarah and the-baby-currently-known-as-Ziggy-but-not-for-long-if-I-could-help-it decided to go back to their hotel for a nap. Probably because of all the sugar she had eaten. It was a relief because (a) now Dad and I could have some alone time, and (b) I felt like my butt was getting bigger just watching Sarah eat.

Dad and I sat on a bench in Madison Square Park, and I suddenly felt like crying again. Sure, we talked on the phone and we e-mailed (although some of the jokes he forwarded on to me were *really* dumb), but just sitting next to him holding his hand with the callouses on the middle and pinky fingers because of the way he held his camera and smelling his smell (a combination of coffee and cinnamon) made me realize again how much I missed him. It wasn't like Alan was a jerk or anything. In fact, as much I had originally thought the whole IBS thing was totally corny, it was working, because not only did I not mind spending time with him, but I actually looked forward to it. Plus, I had gotten an iTouch out of it. But still, my dad had been my dad my entire life.

"Judging from all those texts you keep getting on that fancy iPhone of yours, it seems like you're really starting to build a life for yourself," he said.

"It's an i*Touch*," I corrected him for the fifth time. That was one area where Alan and I were actually a little more bonded than Dad and I were. "There's no phone part to it." I pulled out my cell. "*This* is my phone." Mom said Dad was a Luddite, which meant someone who didn't get e-mail on his phone.

He shook his head and sighed. "Just give me a cordless and an old-style answering machine, and I'm happy." He shifted a little on the bench. "So are any of those texts from . . . *boys*?"

I shifted, too. So much so that I almost fell *off* the bench. "Dad!" I cried. This was almost as embarrassing as when Mom put her hands in my bra to adjust my boobs when we went bra shopping.

"Honey, as much as it terrifies me, I'm fully aware that you're at that age where you're going to start developing those kinds of feelings," he said. "And you know that if they're for a girl instead of a boy, that's perfectly okay, too, right?"

I cringed. I missed hanging with Dad, but if all our time together from now on was going to be filled with these types of conversations, I would've rather just e-mailed with him. The only thing that could make this worse would be if he somehow brought up the phrase *making love*. I hated that phrase. It was so . . . corny. And gross. Even when I got to be an adult, I was never ever going to use it.

"And when you have a crush on someone, I accept the fact that you're going to want to kiss them—at some point," he went on. "Not right away, but at some point," he said nervously. "And that's a beautiful thing. Just like . . . making love is," he said.

I slid down the bench. *PleasepleasepleasePLEASE stop*, I thought to myself.

"Although making love is something you won't experience for *many*, many years," he added.

Okay, that was enough. My parents had sat me down (together, of course, because that's the kind of embarrassing family I came from) when I was eleven to have the Talk about puberty and how babies were made and all that stuff, and of course they used that phrase like nine billion times then. I did not need to sit through this again. "Dad, do you have to keep using that phrase?" I cried.

"What phrase?" he asked. "Making love?"

I slid down even farther. The only good thing about this moment was that it was so embarrassing that hopefully it was bringing on my period. "Yes, that phrase," I said.

"What's wrong with the phrase 'making love'?" he asked, confused.

This time I slunk down so far that I slid off the bench. "Dad! Please!" I was mortified. Didn't he realize people could HEAR him?

"Okay, okay," he said. "So . . . is there anyone . . . *special* in your life?" he asked once I had gotten back up.

I looked at him. I could lie and say no, or I could come clean and tell him about Blair. Unlike SOME people—like, say, the woman who actually gave birth to me—he was interested in hearing about what was going on in my life. Why not? He had once been my age, and also had a good memory on account of all the vitamins Sarah made him take, so he probably could remember what this crush thing was like. And it couldn't hurt to get a boy's opinion on the whole thing. Plus, I was pretty sure there was no way he could work the phrase *making love* into the rest of the conversation.

Weirdly enough, as I was telling him all about Blair and the three-crushes issue, I started to feel . . . lighter. And therefore hungry. At one point Dad yawned, and he kept blinking, like he was having a hard time keeping his eyes open, but I'm pretty sure that was just because the long drive was catching up to him and not because I was boring him. "So what do you think?" I asked when I was finished. "Do you think I have a crush on Blair?"

"I'm not sure," he admitted.

"You're not sure?!" I cried. "But you're an adult—you're supposed to be able to answer these kinds of questions! What should I do?"

Dad shrugged. "Well, there's really not anything *to* do, other than just be yourself and wait for more to be revealed," he said.

What was up with this being yourself stuff?! Didn't my father realize that we were talking about a *boy* here?

He took my hand. "Lucy, relationships are like lotus

flowers. If you allow it to open and blossom at its own rate, you can't go wrong. But if you force it—"

"All the petals will fall off, and it'll get slimy and start to smell really gross because it's rotting?" I said. That's what had happened to the tulips that Alan had bought me at the deli after one of our IBS outings.

He laughed and ruffled my hair, which, both luckily and unluckily, was now long enough to get messed up when it was ruffled. "Yeah, something like that."

I took out my little notebook. That was a good one to write down. It sounded very poetic. Especially the part about the petals falling off.

That night Laurel, Mom, Alan, Dad, Sarah, and I went to dinner at Patsy's Pizzeria on Seventy-fourth Street, which, next to V&T's up on Amsterdam and 110th, was my favorite pizza in the city. And from the way that Sarah ate three garlic knots, two slices of mushroom and pepper, and one slice of cheese, I guess she thought it was pretty delicious, too. Personally, I didn't think it was so weird that we were all eating together, but from the way that Alan dinged his fork on his glass, stood up, and got all choked up as he gave a speech about how grateful he was that the blending was going so smoothly that we were at a point where we could all eat together, I guess he did. Then, after he was done, Dad got up and dinged on *his* glass.

"I feel like I'm at a wedding," I whispered to Laurel.

"I feel like I'm at the Golden Globe Awards," she whispered back.

"Thanks, Alan, for that heartfelt speech," Dad said. "And I, too, am very glad that we're all together today. If fifteen years of studying Buddhism has taught me anything, it's that the only constant in life is change."

Oh great. Another Buddhism lecture from Dad. Now *those* I had not missed. When he delivered them in a public place, they could be very embarrassing.

He reached over and squeezed Mom's hand. "People get divorced." He patted Alan on the shoulder. "But then they fall in love again." I slumped down in my chair as Alan dabbed at his eyes. Dad reached over and patted Sarah's belly as she grabbed for the piece of leftover crust on his plate. He beamed at Laurel and me. "Siblings are born into your life, or they come in later. At any rate, to quote the Dalai Lama, it is all good."

Phew. From having sat through so many of Dad's lectures over the course of my life, I knew that the "It is all good" meant that he was done and we could go back to eating like a semi-normal blended family and stop talking about feelings.

"In fact, even when your daughter tells you that she has her first crush on a boy, it is all good, because that, too, is just part of life."

WHAT?! I almost fell off my chair. What was he *doing*? Did he not realize that there were other people in the room—like, say, my mother?! Obviously, it was her own fault that she didn't already know this information, but still, it's not like I wanted her to find out like *this*.

Everyone turned to me. "You have a crush? You didn't tell me that," Mom said. How was it that with just one little look, I felt like I had been splashed with a giant gallon of guilt? Did they teach moms how to do that in the hospital before they gave birth?

"You told your *dad*?" Laurel asked, surprised.

"A crush?! You have a crush?" Alan asked anxiously. "Who is it on? What does his father do?"

Sarah pointed at my half-eaten slice of pepperoni. "If you're not going to finish that, can I have it?"

"Okay, (a) I'm not even sure it's a crush yet!" I cried. "If you're going to make big announcements, you should at least get the facts right! And (b) I didn't say anything because I kind of thought you'd remember this from when you were a kid, but when someone tells you a *secret*, you're not supposed to then *announce* it to a table full of people!"

"But, honey, these aren't people—this is your *family*!" Dad cried.

I leaned back in my chair as they all started chattering about the crush that I had that I wasn't even sure was a crush as if I wasn't even there. Yes, they were my family, but they were driving me bonkers. At least Laurel and I were leaving for L.A. on Friday, so I'd get a break from them. Dad was always saying that the Buddhists believed that before you were born, you chose the family you were going to come into so you could learn your life lessons. As far as I was concerned, the only lesson I was being forced to learn was how not to die from embarrassment.

I took out my advice notebook. *When you tell a person a secret, make sure you always add the phrase DON'T TELL ANYONE, even if you think that part is super-obvious.*

As I was putting on my old bra that night before bed, there was a knock on my door. But before I could say, "Just a second—don't come in yet," it opened, which meant it was Mom, because she always did that, even though she knew that it totally drove me crazy.

"Lucy, I really wish you'd stop wearing that bra to bed," she said, sitting down on my bed. "It can't be good for your circulation."

"But it's working!" I said. "My boobs are totally shrinking." Okay, maybe they weren't *totally* shrinking, but when I had worn my Angry Little Girls T-shirt the other day, I could have sworn the letters were in a different place.

"So it was nice to see your dad, huh?" she asked, petting Miss Piggy, who had snuggled up in her lap. Why was it that Miss Piggy would let everyone touch her except me? Once I was back from L.A., I was really going to step up my efforts on Operation New Kitten.

"Yeah, it was great," I said, throwing some size-small T-shirts into the pile of "things to be packed for L.A." now that my boobs were deflating. I knew where Mom was going with this. I decided just to cut to the chase. "I'm sorry I didn't tell you about my crush," I mumbled.

"So am I," she said softly. "Look, no one is happier than I am that you have such a great relationship with your dad, but I guess I'm just a little hurt that you didn't tell me, too."

She was hurt? What about me? I'd tried to tell her about the crush, but she'd been ignoring me for weeks! "Well, maybe if you weren't so busy all the time, I would have," I blurted out.

"What are you talking about?" she asked, confused.

"I'm talking about the fact that ever since we moved here, you're either going on fun IBSs with Laurel, or hanging out with venus, or looking for places to get married, or totally forgetting about me when I tell you I have something to talk to you about," I replied.

"Lucy, I—"

My eyes started to get glassy. "You know, just because you've known me for twelve years doesn't mean you can stop bonding with me, too."

She got really quiet, and *her* eyes filled with tears, too. Jeez. No wonder why I cried so much—it was hereditary. "I guess you're right," she said quietly. "I think because I was so afraid of anyone feeling left out, or of there being an us-versus-them dynamic, I went too far the other way."

She sighed. "I think because you're so strong I somehow didn't think about how it was affecting you."

I looked up from the crumpled mound of "to be packed" clothes that were getting more wrinkled by the moment. Luckily, Laurel really enjoyed ironing— maybe I could get her to iron my stuff when we got to the hotel. "'Strong?' Mom, I fail the Presidential Physical Fitness Tests every year in gym." I hated gym. Most of the time I skipped it by using the "Please excuse Lucy B. Parker from gym today on account of the fact that she is menstruating" note that Marissa had forged for me.

She laughed. "I meant emotionally strong," she said. "And you're so resilient."

"Can you just speak in English, please?" I sighed. "I'm too tired to turn on my computer and look stuff up on dictionary.com."

She took my hands in hers. "Resilient means being able to bounce back to your original form. Like after the divorce. Or when Rachel and Missy ended their friendship with you. Or when you burned your hair off. Or when I told you we were going to have to move to New York if we were going to make a family with Alan and Laurel—"

I cringed. She just listed the greatest hits of the horrible things that had happened to me. Way to make a person feel better.

"After all those things, you could've gotten really

angry and just stayed in your room all the time and cried and not talked to anyone. But you didn't."

"That's not true," I corrected her. "I stayed in my room and cried a lot. Remember, you yelled at me for using so many of the Cold Care tissues?" They were the best ones because they were super-soft, so your nose didn't get all red, but they were also expensive.

"I mean that you cried for a while, but when you were done, you got up and brushed yourself off and held your head high and went back out into the world," she said. "You never lost your ... Lucyness."

My Lucyness? What did *that* mean? That I wore a lot of color? That I overshared? That I tripped a lot because of my coordination problem? "Maybe I seem strong and re—what was that word again?"

"Resilient," Mom said.

"Resilient ... but I'm still a kid. Even if I *am* about to get my period any day now. Do you have any idea how much my neck hurts from holding my head up? Or how many tissues I've *really* gone through? Or how many times I had to go hide in the bathroom stall at school to cry? Being twelve hasn't been very fun," I said, starting to cry again.

Mom reached over and handed me a tissue and then grabbed one for herself. "I know it hasn't. And I'm sorry for not realizing that as precocious and resilient as you may be, you still very much need your mother." She reached over and hugged me. "But I need you to do something for me, okay? Instead of letting this get all bottled up, I need you to talk to me about it. And I'm going to make a really big effort so that when you say, 'Mom, I need to talk to you,' I'm going to put aside whatever I'm doing to listen, okay?"

I nodded.

"And when you get back from L.A., you and I will have an extra-special IBS session, okay?"

"No doctor or dentist appointments," I warned. "Or bra shopping."

She laughed. "No doctor or dentist appointments or bra shopping. I'm thinking maybe even a weekend away—just the two of us."

I nodded as I burrowed deeper into her arms. I may have been only twelve—closer to thirteen, in fact—but at that moment, I definitely wasn't too old to have my mom hug me. "Mom? Can I ask you something?"

"Of course."

"Can I get a kitten now?"

She laughed. "Nice try. No."

I sighed. Obviously, she didn't feel *that* bad for me.

chapter 6

Dear Dr. Maude,

You're not going to believe this, but I am sending you this e-mail FROM THE AIRPLANE!!! From somewhere over Illinois, actually, because the captain just said, "Folks, we're just passing over Chicago, Illinois." I'm sure you know this already, because you're very famous and fly all the time, but if you have a credit card (I don't, but Laurel does), you can pay $12.95 and be on the Internet for the entire flight!

I'm sure because of the famous thing you get to sit in first class, too, but in case you don't, it's really REALLY cool. First of all, the seats are a lot bigger and cushier than the ones in the regular part of the plane, so you don't feel like your butt is getting all bruised. And as soon as you sit down, they offer you something to drink. For free, BTW! And then when it's time for lunch, the food comes on real plates rather than in those plastic TV dinner–looking things. Also for free!

Oh, and every seat has its own movie screen so you can watch whatever you want. Laurel's watching Austin Mackenzie's latest movie, *Surfing Safari*, the one where he surfs with a chimp—and is getting all googly-eyed because, unlike me, she KNOWS she has a crush on him. If the actual L.A. part of the trip is half as good as the plane ride, I'll be happy—especially if I get to be on your show. (I don't mean to be a pain or anything, but have you thought any more about that?) When we get to L.A., we're staying at a fancy hotel in Santa Monica called Shutters on the Beach, and it's literally ON THE BEACH. According to Laurel, you can hear the waves from your room and everything!

Plus, when we get to the airport, a LIMOUSINE is picking us up, and apparently they have water and little candies in the back that you can have. Also for free! It's kind of weird that people pay all this money to go first class only to then get a bunch of free stuff with it, but I'm not complaining. In fact, I'm not sure if I'll get to do this again, so I'm making sure to take as many souvenirs as I can (I took three of the little hand lotion bottles from the airplane bathroom already).

I do have to say, this is the first time I've seen Laurel in full Laurel-Moses-teen-superstar mode—you know, not trying to hide the Movie-Star thing—and it's kind of weird. It's not like she's being mean to me or anything like that, but for once she's definitely not trying to hide the fact that she's famous like she does in New York. It makes me a little nervous, because she's acting all weird. But I'm sure everything will be fine. Right?

Okay, I have to go because the flight attendant just brought me the soda I asked for and I don't want to spill it on my laptop. You know, because of my coordination issues.

yours truly,
LUCY B. PARKER

When you're a person with coordination issues, being blinded by flashes from the paparazzi as you try to make your way through an airport doesn't help. If anything, it makes you stumble around as if you're playing Helen Keller in a school play.

"How'd they even know you were here?" I asked Laurel, rubbing my eyes to try to unblind myself as we climbed into the limo that was going to take us to Shutters.

"Marci tipped them off," Laurel replied. Marci was Laurel's publicist. I had never met her because she lived in L.A., but I would when she came to the set on Monday. According to Laurel, most publicists were Mean Girl types, sort of like Cristina Pollock. Which is why they were good at spreading gossip, like, say, when a star landed at an airport. Laurel didn't like Marci all that much ("Because, like, she talks in questions?" she said. "Like this?"), but apparently having a publicist was just as important as having an agent or a personal assistant or a psychic—all of which Laurel had. Her assistant was named Jaycee, and although I hadn't met her yet, I had talked to her on the phone. And her psychic was named Gorgeous George. I was *dying* to meet him.

Back in New York, Marci was usually trying to keep the paparazzi *away* from Laurel—not lead them to her. "Why would she do that?" I asked, glancing at the limo driver to make sure he wasn't looking before I shoved more mints in my bag.

"Because this is such an important role for me—you know, because of the kissing and stuff," she explained. "She wants to use this movie to help me change my image so that people start seeing me in a more grown-up way. And the pictures of me will be on gossip websites and in magazines and stuff."

As we pulled up to the hotel, and I saw the swarm of paparazzi standing in front of the entrance, I started to get nervous. I knew that Laurel was getting tired of being considered America's Sweetheart because of her show, but did she have to pick this trip to change everything? How were we going to bond with photographers and people around all the time? And what if she ended up totally forgetting about me and I ended up spending all my time examining the ends of my hair? Which was something I did when I had nothing to do but wanted to make it look like I had something to do.

As the limo driver opened my door, I took a deep breath. At least my hair had grown out enough that if I ended up in any of those pictures I wouldn't look like a giant egghead.

Once we got in the lobby of the hotel, Mr. Patel, the concierge of the hotel (a fancy way of saying the guy who's in charge and gets to boss everyone else around in a very polite voice), told us the bad news: there had been a screwup, and there wasn't a regular suite available. But the good news was that we were going to be in the Presidential Suite!

"Has the president actually stayed in it?" I asked Mr. Patel, while Laurel signed autographs and posed for pictures for people and said things like, "No, it's a pleasure to meet *you*!" in the higher-than-normal voice she used when she was being Laurel-Moses-teen-superstar.

"I'm not at liberty to say, Miss Parker," he replied in a polite English accent, as he led us into the elevator and up to the top floor. Laurel had gotten back on the phone, which, frankly, I thought was pretty rude, but I didn't say anything. It didn't seem very polite to get into a fight with someone in front of a very polite person like Mr. Patel. When he showed us the room, I gasped. It was a bajillion times nicer than the rooms at Disney World's Port Orleans French Quarter, which, up until then, was the nicest hotel I had ever stayed in. This suite had two bedrooms, two bathrooms with huge Jacuzzi bathtubs, a kitchen, a dining room table that sat six people, a huge flat-screen TV, a fireplace, and a view of the Pacific Ocean right outside the window. Even though I was really excited to see L.A., I would've been happy to spend the entire week inside watching DVDs.

I walked over to the ginormous Welcome-to-Shutters, we-hope-you-enjoy-your-stay welcome basket. "Hey, Laurel—check this out!" I said.

"Lucy, I'm on the phone," she whispered.

Chocolate-covered almonds?! Peanut-butter pretzels?! Saltwater taffy?! The basket was packed with the best foods! The only thing missing were red velvet cupcakes. I turned to Mr. Patel. "Is this free, or does it cost money like the stuff in the minibar?" Mom had warned me that under no circumstances was I allowed to eat the stuff from the minibar, because they charged you like ten bucks for a candy bar.

"That's complimentary, Miss Parker," he replied politely, as he walked around and adjusted vases that were already perfect and straightened piles of magazines that were already straight. Complimentary meant FREE.

I grabbed some peanut-butter pretzels, flopped down on the couch, and turned on the big-screen TV. "Laurel, look—*Pretty in Pink* is on!" I said. It was a really old movie, but we both loved it. In fact, it was one of the first things we had bonded over after I moved to New York.

"Lucy, I told you—I'm on the phone. Now please be quiet," she said in a very un-Laurel-like, unpolite way, shooting me a mean look.

I couldn't believe she was treating me like some sort of annoying little sister. Way to embarrass me in front of Mr. Patel. Luckily, when I glanced over at him, he was busy fluffing pillows on the other couch across the room, so he probably hadn't heard or seen her look, but still, I was totally embarrassed.

I stood up and turned off the TV. "Fine. I'll just go into the other room then," I grumbled.

I waited for her to say something like, "No, Lucy, don't go. Please stay. I'm sorry I snapped at you like that," but she didn't. Instead, she just kept yakking away on her stupid phone.

Once Laurel finally got off the phone and unpacked and ironed her clothes (I decided in light of the weirdness that was going on not to ask her to iron mine), she seemed to relax a little bit, and things got back to normal between us. After ordering pancakes for dinner from room service (that was one of the best things about room service—breakfast at dinnertime), which we ate on our private deck overlooking the Pacific Ocean, I was ready to conk out. Between the sea air and the super-comfortable bed with the softest sheets I had ever felt in my life, I slept like a log, and

I was relieved that when I woke up the next morning, Laurel was back to being plain old Laurel instead of Laurel-Moses-teen-superstar-who-is-on-the-phone-all-the-time.

She didn't have to start work on the movie set until Monday, so we had two whole days to sightsee, which was awesome—especially since "sightseeing" with Laurel was done in a chauffeured car with a guy who knew where he was going, instead of Dad, who had to pull over every few minutes to look at a map. I could get used to this no-parents thing. We went to Grauman's Chinese Theatre, and I got to see the handprints and footprints. Then we drove to the Venice boardwalk and watched all the weirdos like the guy with dreadlocks who roller-skated around in what looked like a bikini bottom while playing an electric guitar, and this woman who painted pictures using ketchup and mustard for five dollars.

On Sunday, we went on a super-fancy private tour of Universal Studios, and when we got back to the hotel, we got these amazing burgers delivered from this place called Father's Office. I was finishing my burger when Laurel started freaking out and getting really nervous about the fact that in less than twenty-four hours she would be meeting her crush, Austin Mackenzie. And within a week, she'd have to *kiss* him. In front of an entire film crew. A bunch of times.

"Look at the bright side," I said, as she paced around

the suite. "You have a crush on him, so pretending you want to kiss him shouldn't be too hard. If you want, I'll run lines with you so you can practice. It'll be like . . . studying for a kissing quiz."

She stopped pacing. "Really? You'd do that?"

Would I do that?! I had been dying to do that! I had just been too shy to ask before this. It's not like I wanted to be an actress (see "not even able to get a role as a munchkin in the school play" for further details), especially because acting called for things like coordination and memorization and talent, and all I was good at was blurting, tripping, and keeping track of girls' periods (and maybe crushes, but the crush log was still too new to tell for sure). But still, it was a way to get a little taste of what it was like to be a famous actor.

She thrust her script at me. "Here—you be Austin."

"I don't want to be the *boy*," I said. It's like when I used to play Barbies with Rachel and Missy and they'd make me be Ken. I was hoping to be someone... interesting. Like the great-grandmother character. Laurel let me look at the script a while back, and I had thought she was a really funny character. And when Laurel said that Lady Countess Annabel Ashcroft de Winter von Taxi, one of the greatest actresses of all time, was going to play her, I was completely psyched. I was *dying* to meet her. I had read on Wikipedia that she had started out in the theater in London, but now she played the grandmother or great-aunt with magical powers in almost every movie that had a wizard or a witch or a vampire.

"But we're doing this so I can practice my scenes with Austin, remember?"

"Oh yeah," I said. As we went over her lines, every time we got to the part where I said, in what I thought was a very Austin-like voice, "Wow—that potion I cooked up seems to have worked, because I think I'm standing in front of my soul mate," she just stared at me all googly-eyed, and I'd have to snap my fingers and say, "Um, hi, Earth to Laurel—now you're supposed to say, 'Oh Henry—I bet you say that to all the girls!'"

She flopped back on her bed, which, because it was something called a California king, was even bigger than Mom and Alan's bed back in New York. "I can't do this," she moaned.

"Yes, you can. If you want, we can make cue cards, or you can write the lines on your hand." The writing-on-the-hand thing worked really well for me when I had to give oral reports. Well, as long as I didn't get nervous to the point where my palms started to sweat. Then, not so much.

"No—all of this with Austin!" she cried. "Who am I kidding, thinking he's going to like me back? He's *Austin Mackenzie*, and I'm just—"

"One of the biggest stars in the world and one of *Teen People*'s Most Beautiful People just like him?" I finished.

"Yes, but if we really get to know each other, then he'll see that underneath all that I'm just ... *me*."

"And the problem with that is ...?"

"That I'm a total dork!" she cried.

It still amazed me that no matter how many awards she won, or how many e-mails she got from fans, Laurel was just as insecure as every other girl in the world. Well, except for Cristina Pollock, who seemed to be absent the day they were handing that part out. "You're not a total dork," I said. "I mean, sure, you can be a *little* bit dorkish sometimes—like with the organizing and the making sure everything is buttoned when you hang it on a hanger—but I'm sort of a dork, too. That's why we get along so well."

Although I felt awful admitting this, I was kind of glad that Laurel was a bit of a dork. Because the whole acting-like-a-movie-star thing had made me feel a little worried—like soon enough, she'd realize she was just as fabulous as everyone thought she was, and then she wouldn't want to be my friend anymore.

She smiled at me. "I guess you're right."

"Plus, you're now in the same city with the guy who's your local, long-distance, *and* celebrity crush. Not many people can say that. I bet it brings you a ton of luck."

"I hope so." She smiled at me. A regular-Laurel smile, not a superstar-Laurel one. "I'm really glad you're here with me, Lucy."

"Me, too," I said as I smiled back a Lucy smile, which is the only kind I had.

On Monday morning, Laurel worked out with the personal trainer that the producers of the movie had gotten her, so I walked to this place called Urth Caffé on Main Street for breakfast. Laurel said that hardly anyone walked anywhere in L.A., and as I walked down Pico Boulevard and made a left on Main Street, I discovered that she was right. I didn't pass a single person other than a homeless guy and a woman in a fur coat (even though it was June) and sunglasses (even though it was cloudy) walking a little yippy dog that also had sunglasses on.

It was still pretty early, but the café was packed with very beautiful, very smiley people. A lot of them were wearing yoga outfits. Sarah would've loved it. Well, she would've loved it back before she got pregnant. Now she would've been more interested in the delicious-looking muffins and cookies behind the glass display.

"Did I hear you right?" asked Brandi, my waitress. "You really want the Bread Pudding Breakfast?"

I nodded and pointed to the menu. "It says right here that it's 'the best breakfast in L.A.'" Lots of times menus tried to make things sound better than they were, but how could bread pudding with baked bananas on top *not* be good?

"Yeah, but no one actually . . . *orders* it," she replied. "It's so . . . *bready*. You sure you don't want an egg white omelet like that guy over there?" she asked, motioning to a man at the next table reading a newspaper called *Variety*, which I knew from Laurel and Alan was the daily paper for people in the movie business. "Or some yogurt and fruit like her?" she asked, pointing to a woman next to him reading the *Hollywood Reporter*, which was the other movie-business newspaper.

I wrinkled my nose. Even someone like me, who wasn't so great at math, knew that "no adults around" plus "dessert-sounding breakfast" equaled "must order." And "egg whites" plus "fruit" equaled "way boring." "No, thank you," I said. "I'm going to try the best breakfast in L.A."

My food arrived, and while I wasn't sure how it stacked up against other restaurants in L.A., it was pretty delicious—especially when I asked for a side of peanut butter to smear on it. "What a marvelous sight!" came an English accent from behind me. "It's not often in this town that you see a young girl enjoying her food with such . . . *relish*. How utterly refreshing!"

Oh my God. I'd recognize that voice anywhere—it had been in almost every single one of my favorite movies! I whipped around and gasped. It was her! Right in front of me was Lady Countess Annabel Ashcroft de Winter von Taxi! She was even wearing her trademark turban and a long flowy robe-looking dress, which Mom had once told me was called a caftan, so she looked just like she did in her pictures.

Except maybe a little older. I leaned forward for a better look. Okay, maybe a *lot* older.

"I can't believe Lady Countess Annabel Ashcroft de Winter von Taxi just called me utterly refreshing!" I squealed. I looked down at her plate, where some leftover pancake was floating in syrup. "And you eat bread, too!" Pancakes weren't technically bread, but they were in the bread family.

She gave one of her long tinkly laughs and sounded just like she did in *Wizard Academy.* "Of course, I do, darling. Life is not worth living without bread—never forget that. It's as important to remember as taking your makeup off before you go to sleep, no matter how many scotches you've had to drink."

I scrambled to pull my advice notebook out of my bag. "Would you mind repeating that, please?" I asked. "I recently started keeping a notebook of advice, and I think that definitely needs to be in there."

She gave another tinkly laugh. "An *advice* book! How *marvelous*! I do hope that the young girl, what's-her-name, who is playing my great-granddaughter in the movie I'm about to do, is as wonderful as you."

"Oh, she is," I said. I couldn't believe I was talking to Lady Countess Annabel Ashcroft de Winter von Taxi in person! Laurel was famous, but Lady Countess Annabel Ashcroft de Winter von Taxi was FAMOUS-famous. The whole thing was making me nervous. I just hoped I didn't start sweating under my arms, because that would've been super-embarrassing.

"You know her, dear?"

I nodded. "Our bedrooms are right next to each other. She's my frister. That's a combination friend/sister," I explained.

"I love it!" she boomed. "What a marvelous word!" She leaned in. "So she's not like that girl I worked with on *Sister Swap*—the one who ended up getting in all that trouble with the law?"

I knew who she was talking about—Taylor Tompkins, whose mug shot seemed to be on the cover of the gossip magazines every week because she was always getting arrested. "Oh no—Laurel's like the complete opposite," I replied, relaxing a little. Lady Countess Annabel Ashcroft de Winter von Taxi was so nice it was hard to remember to be nervous. "She's *so* nice. And pretty boring compared to most stars. I mean, her idea of a fun Friday night is alphabetizing her bookshelf and making labels for file folders."

She smiled. "Well, as long as everyone is aware that it's in my contract that I get more close-ups than she does, I'm sure we'll get along just fine." She stood up. "Sadly, darling, I must get going. As I get older, they seem to keep me a little bit longer in the makeup chair with each movie. I do hope you'll drop by to say hello if you come to the set."

"Actually, I'll be there later today!" I said excitedly. Maybe Lady Countess Annabel Ashcroft de Winter von

Taxi could help me out with this crush stuff. A woman who had been married six times had to know a lot about boys.

"Magnifique!" she cried, which I knew from Beatrice was French for "Magnificent!" She leaned down and kissed me on both cheeks. "Ta for now, then!" she trilled as she walked out.

"Ta!" I trilled back. Unfortunately, because I wasn't used to trilling, I ended up spitting all over myself.

If the rest of the trip was this exciting, I'd definitely be getting my period, because according to Marissa, excitement—in addition to embarrassment and drama—was also known to bring it on.

chapter 7

Dear Dr. Maude,

GUESS where I am right now? You probably won't guess, so I'll just tell you. In the car on the way to Olympus Studios! Don't worry—I'm not coming to stalk you. I'm going to the set of Laurel's movie. Anyway, the reason I am writing this to you now is because, as usual, I need some advice.

Remember how I told you that Laurel was acting all movie star–like when we got to L.A.? Well, first things got better over the weekend, but now it's gotten worse. WAY worse. She's been on the phone pretty much nonstop with her manager, and her agent, and her publicist, on account of the fact that even though she hasn't even shot the kissing scene with Austin Mackenzie, there's all this buzz around Hollywood about how awesome she is in the movie (which they haven't even started shooting yet!) and how it shows a whole new side to her, and suddenly she's getting all these offers for other movies. And I get that this is her job and all, but every time I say, "Um, Laurel?" she gives this annoyed sigh before she says, "What, Lucy?" and sounds just like Mom does after I've been asking her a lot of questions. She didn't even listen when I tried to tell her about meeting Lady

Countess Annabel Ashcroft de Winter von Taxi at breakfast this morning. (Is that not the best celebrity sighting ever? Not only that, but she LOVES the fact that I eat bread, because apparently not many people here in L.A. do.)

Do you have any advice about what I should do to fix this? Because I still have five days to go, and if I wanted to be ignored all the time, I could have stayed in New York.

yours truly,
Lucy B. Parker

Even with Laurel back to being kind of a jerk, I was still excited to be in Hollywood. As we drove down Melrose Avenue, I looked out the window and gasped. "Oh my God! There's the Hollywood sign!" I yelled.

Laurel barely glanced up from her phone. "Huh? Oh. Yeah." She went back to e-mailing or whatever she was doing, other than ignoring me.

My face got hot, and I slid down in my seat. I probably sounded like a total tourist. But I *was* a tourist! And therefore it was okay to act like one. Just because *she* had seen the Hollywood sign nine million times didn't mean *I* couldn't get excited about it.

Her phone rang again. She looked at the screen. "It's Howard—I need to take it," she said.

I sighed as I slumped back against the seat. She

"needed" to take every call—from Howard, from Marci, from Jaycee. But what she really needed to do was stop acting like she was some famous star. Even though she was. As she yakked away, I looked out the window and took in the sights. Palm trees, shiny fancy cars that didn't have any scratches or dings like Dad's old Saab did, more yippy dogs with sunglasses. At least I had interesting things to look at while I was being ignored.

Finally, the limo drove through a pair of iron gates and I shouted, "Oh my God—I can't believe I'm at the world-famous Olympus Studios!" Laurel gave me a Do-you-not-see-I'm-on-the-phone-so-can-you-PLEASE-keep-it-down? look.

"Sorry," I mumbled, slumping back down.

Once the limo let us out and Laurel and I walked to the hair and makeup trailer, we passed a bunch of buildings that kind of looked like New York City (it had a bodega and everything), but brighter and cleaner. Laurel explained that they were sets, and because they shot lots of movies and TV shows at Olympus, there were lots of different kinds. We saw one that was supposed to look like the Wild West (no bodegas there—just a saloon) and one that Laurel said was supposed to be Paris on account of the fact that the signs were all in French. Not only that, but all the people we passed were dressed in different costumes. It was like Halloween, but with grown-ups smoking cigarettes and drinking Red Bull.

Every time we passed a truck, I'd say, "Is *that* the craft services truck?" because (a) I was dying to see one in person and (b) I was hungry. But Laurel was too busy texting to answer me. Finally, we got to a trailer that said LAUREL MOSES—HAIR & MAKEUP, and she turned to me. "The producer wants to see me, so I'm going to leave you with Roger and Maya, okay?"

Fine with me. At least *they'd* be nice to me. The first time I had met them, back in Northampton, Roger had fixed the haircut that Mom's friend Deanna had given me after the Straightening Iron Incident, and Maya had given me a makeover. After a round of hugs, Maya gave me the once-over. "Your hair is really growing," she said.

"Yeah, I guess," I sighed. "But it's still not anywhere close to being down to my butt," I said.

Roger clucked. "But I see *someone* decided to cut her bangs herself."

Laurel had warned me about how upset Roger got if you touched your own hair. And an angry bald man covered with tattoos was sort of a scary sight. "Sorry. It's just that they were really getting in my eyes." That plus coordination issues equaled lots of bumping into things.

"Sit," he said, pointing to the chair. "I need to do some damage control." After he fixed my bangs, he decided to give me a full trim. "So what's new and exciting?" he asked, snipping away. "How are things going with you and Laurel?" One of the only reasons I'd want to be famous was so that I could have someone do my hair every day. Well, that, and the baked goods baskets that Laurel said people sent you when you were nominated for awards.

I shrugged. "They're fine."

He stood back to look at my hair. He was only halfway done, and already I looked much better. I looked definitely thirteen instead of twelve and a half. He turned to Maya. "Let's give her a little blush, shall we?"

Maya pulled out some brushes and little jars and started dusting blush on my cheekbones. Mom thought I was too young for makeup, and I didn't really like it anyway because it felt sticky and I usually ended up smearing it on account of my coordination issue, but (a) Mom wasn't around because she, too, had dumped me, and (b) it's not like I had anything better to do. "I hate to tell you this, honey, but that was not a very believable-sounding 'fine,'" she said.

I sighed. Even though Roger and Maya worked for Laurel and not me, I felt close enough to tell them what was going on with Laurel. "Well, the minute we got to L.A., Laurel went from Laurel-normal-girl to Laurel-Moses-teen-superstar. And even though she'd been totally normal all weekend, now she's on the phone all the time, and she keeps shushing me and acting like I'm totally embarrassing her like some dorky younger sister just because I'm all excited about being in Hollywood. And when I try to talk to her about something important"—like, say, about whether she thought that what I had on Blair was a crush-crush or a fake-crush—"instead of paying attention to what I'm saying, she's texting with Marci." Saying all of it out loud made me realize how used I had become to having Laurel in my life. I had really come to depend on her as a frister . . . which is why this change in her bummed me out so much. I could feel the tears start welling and snuffled to keep them down.

"Oh honey, that happens every few months—usually when she's working on a movie instead of the show," Roger said.

"Yeah, you know how everyone on TV really just wants to be a movie star?" said Maya.

Roger fiddled with my hair some more. "She's got a lot riding on this. But don't worry—she'll stop soon enough," he said.

"Really? You think so?" I asked. I wasn't so sure. "Because I'm feeling like a total tagalong." This must have been what Marissa and Alice must feel like on account that they *were* tagalongs. Oh no—was I Laurel's Marissa? Was she sitting there that very moment telling the producer how annoying I was? Was she just being a really good actress all those times she said she was glad I was there with her and pretending to be nice to me because she thought it would help her karma or something?

Roger put some product in my hair. "I don't think so—I *know* so. That girl could soon enough survive without you nowadays as she could without the two of us," he said. Wow. I didn't want to sound conceited, but my hair looked *really* good. Like, so good I didn't even put my purple flower back on (I had kind of become addicted to wearing it). "And believe me, I'm a hairdresser—we know about these things."

After a half hour sitting on the film set, I took out my advice notebook. *If you ever get to go on a film set, make sure you bring a book to read, because next to watching your frister organize her sock drawer, it's the second most boring thing in the world.* I'd been on a film set only once before, back in Northampton, but even though I'd been there for only five minutes before the Hat Incident, it had seemed pretty interesting. But it turned out that Laurel *was* right—all you did was wait. For the gaffers (the guys who handle the lighting) to fix the lights. For the camera people to move the cameras. For the movie director to fight with the director of photography about where the lights and cameras should be set up.

And to make everything worse, within my first hour there, I had ruined three shots. The first when, not knowing the director had called "Action," I had scraped my chair on the ground as I was moving it in order to get a better view. The second because I had yelled, "I don't think these headphones are working" (you had to wear headphones to hear what was going on because the actors were so far away, and so they piped in the sound from the giant fuzzy microphone, which was called a

boom, that was hanging above them)—again, not knowing the director had already called "Action." And the
third because I had accidentally walked into the frame
when I was coming back from the bathroom.

I was seriously considering going back there to hide
when I saw Marci walk on set. Laurel had described
her perfectly—perfectly blow-dried red hair, super-high
heels, her mouth all puckered like she had just sucked
on a lemon—and even though Laurel had said that
Marci wasn't nice, I smiled. Finally—someone to talk to.
"You must be Marci," I said after she *click-clacked* over to
where I was sitting.

"I am. And you would be . . . ?" she snapped.

"Lucy B. Parker," I said, holding out my hand. "Laurel's
frister. That's a combination friend/sister."

"Oh—you're *that* Lucy? Her *stepsister*?" she demanded
as her fingers flew across the keyboard of her iPhone.
She didn't even bother to look at me. My smile faded.
The way she said *stepsister* sounded like it was a disease or something. After that I didn't even bother to
try to talk to her, even though she sat right next to me
on set. As soon as Laurel was done doing her scene
with Lady Countess Annabel Ashcroft de Winter von
Taxi (who didn't see me waving at her, and went back
to her trailer before I even got a chance to go over and
say hi), Marci rushed up to her and started chattering away, leaving me alone. Again. Laurel didn't even
look my way or anything.

As I sat there trying not to pick my cuticles, even though it was a nervous habit and I was very nervous about sitting there by myself, looking like a loser, a bald guy, who looked to be Alan's age, with ears that looked like jug handles, plopped down in the folding chair beside me. "Hi. I'm Sylvester Benjamin-Morgan," he said in an English accent.

"Hello. I'm Lucy B. Parker," I replied.

"So are you one of the actresses in the movie?" he asked.

I snorted. "No way. I'm just here to support Laurel Moses. We're fr—almost stepsisters."

His eyes lit up. "Oh really," he said. "So, Lucy B. Parker. What's that like?"

Finally—someone to talk to. I was so happy not to feel completely invisible, and so wanted to keep him there as long as possible so I didn't feel like a total friendless loser, that I started at the beginning—about the Hat Incident and how I really didn't like Laurel after that, but then how we bonded at the ice-cream place, and about how I took her to the mall because she hadn't been to one before. Occasionally, he'd jot something down on the little notebook in his lap, which seemed a little weird, but I knew from movies that English people were really smart, so he was probably the kind of person who was always taking notes so they could study all the time.

As I was telling him about how organized Laurel

was, Marci came *click-clacking* over. "*What* are you doing here, Sylvester?" she demanded. "I told you there was no way I would allow you access to Laurel?"

"Oh wow—you two know each other?" I asked.

"Know each other? Sylvester Benjamin-Morgan is only *the* sleaziest tabloid reporter in all of Great Britain?" she yelled. Was she telling me? Or asking me?

I could feel my face getting hot. Oh no. I had totally screwed up.

"I'd say 'sleazy' is a bit strong, love," he said, as he backed away from her, and then took off running.

Laurel walked over to us, and the knot that was forming in my stomach got tighter. "What's going on?" Laurel asked.

Oh double no. Laurel hated the sleazy tabloids even more than an unorganized drawer. "Nothing. I was just—" I started to say, my voice quivering.

"She was just giving an interview to Sylvester Benjamin-Morgan?" Marci said.

Laurel paled. "You were what?"

"I wasn't giving an interview to him!" I cried. "I was just talking to him."

"About what?" she demanded.

"About...us. How we met and stuff," I said nervously. Maybe Marci had been exaggerating—maybe Sylvester wasn't from a sleazy tabloid. Maybe he was from *People* or *US Weekly*. That would only be partially-bad instead of bad-bad.

"Lucy, he's the one who wrote the story about how I was an alien from another planet," Laurel said.

Oh, this was definitely bad-bad. I slunk down in my chair so far I fell off it completely. Marci turned to Laurel. "Didn't you tell her that she's never to talk to reporters without an adult present?"

Oh, please. Marci was only twenty-four. That was hardly an adult.

"I didn't know I was talking to a reporter!" I said, swiping at my eyes, which were now filled with tears. "I just thought I was talking to . . . I don't know . . . someone who was being *friendly* to me."

"I can't believe you did that, Lucy! My dad is going to freak when he hears this!" Laurel was turning purple she was so mad, which was one of the few colors she didn't look good in.

"It's not like I did it on purpose!" I yelled, the tears really coming now. I reached into my pocket, but all I found was a scratchy napkin from Starbucks instead of a soft tissue.

Marci pointed into the distance toward a short bald guy with glasses. "Laurel, there's the writer from *In Touch with People*? You need to go talk to him? You can yell at her later?"

Before I could say, "But it was a mistake—I don't deserve to be yelled at!" or even "How many times do you want me to say it? I'm *sorry*," the two of them had stomped off.

This wasn't fair. It wasn't my fault that everything was going from bad to worse . . . very quickly. After I wiped my eyes with the bottom of my shirt, I took out my advice notebook. *When you're offered a trip to Hollywood, remember to SAY NO!!* I wrote.

When I get nervous—like, say, about what my stepfather-to-be-who-gets-super-paranoid-about-what-people-say-to-sleazy-tabloid-journalists-about-his-superstar-daughter is going to do when he finds out that I was talking to one of them—I get hungry. Which is why, as Laurel talked to the non-sleazy journalist and Marci shot me dirty looks, I decided to set out to find craft services. Even though I was probably going to get yelled at again later for leaving the set without telling anyone, I just snuck away, because (a) I couldn't get Laurel's attention because she was too busy flipping her hair and laughing louder than normal talking to the reporter, and (b) it's not like Laurel would care that I was gone anyway.

There weren't any cabs or buses to mow you down at the studio like there were in Manhattan, but there were lots of golf carts carrying suit-wearing people screaming into their cell phones that I had to dodge instead. And there were guys on top of ginormous cranes with lights and cameras on the end of them who screamed, "Hey kid—watch where you're going!"when I almost ran into them as I was jumping out of the way of the golf carts. And there was a guy wearing sunglasses who kind-of, sort-of looked like this very famous actor who starred in lots of action-adventure movies, who turned to a bodyguard-looking guy next to him and yelled, "Please tell that girl to stop staring at me—you know how I hate that!" It was like being on a dangerous obstacle course. I was so busy trying to save my own life, I stopped crying, but ten minutes later, after no luck in finding craft services, I decided just to turn around and go back in the direction I had come. Except because I don't really *have* any sense of direction, I couldn't figure out which way that was. As I walked, instead of the city street scenes and cranes I had passed on my way there, all I saw were buildings that didn't look familiar at all.

And then...there it was.

Written in the same big red letters that flashed across my TV screen every day was a big sign on one of the warehouses that said COME ON, PEOPLE—GET WITH THE PROGRAM—AUDIENCE ENTRANCE.

When Sarah said yogalike things like, "Everything happens for a reason" and "Coincidence is the Universe's way of remaining anonymous," I usually rolled my eyes. But at that moment, I realized that my no-sense-of-direction issue was a *good* thing, because without it, I'd be back on set getting yelled at or being ignored, instead of about to have all my problems solved so I'd never have a bad day ever again!

I'm not one to cut, but instead of going to the back of the huge line of people wearing TOLEDO LOVES DR. MAUDE or BUCK UP OR SHUT UP T-shirts, I marched up to the security guard at the front.

"Hi. My name is Lucy B. Parker, and if it's not too much trouble, I'd very much appreciate it if you could let Dr. Maude know that I'm out here," I said politely.

The guard snorted. "Yeah, right, kid. Now either get to the back of the line or be on your way, okay?" He flashed a smile. "And have a nice day."

"But you don't understand. I *really* need some advice from her," I said.

He pointed to the line of people. "Yeah, and so do all these people."

"But she and I are e-mail friends! She knows I'm coming!" I cried. It was maybe half a lie, as I was pretty sure the other person had to be writing you back in order to be e-mail friends, but not a *total* lie. And she did know I was coming. Well, she knew if she actually read the e-mails.

He rolled his eyes. "Like I haven't heard *that* one before. Now come on—back of the line or leave."

I leaned in. "Seriously—you have *no idea* how much advice I need at the moment. I may only be twelve and a half, but I have as much going on in my life as an adult in a telenovela at the moment. See, first my parents got divorced. And then my dad started dating this weird yoga teacher, and now they're having a baby, and they're naming him Ziggy, if you can believe that—"

"My uncle's name is Ziggy," he said.

"—which is a really cool name," I continued, in hopes of getting on his good side. "And then my mom fell in love with a guy whose daughter happens to be"—I had learned my lesson: there was no way I was going to mention Laurel by name to ANYONE from now on—"a superstar. And then I had to move to New York City. And then, to make matters worse, according to Beatrice—she's my new best friend—I found out that I have to have not only one, but *three* crushes—"

He pointed to the line. "Look, if you go stand there, you'll probably be able to get tickets for one of the tapings two weeks from now—"

"But there's more!" I cried. I hadn't even gotten to the part about Mom abandoning me because I'm so resilient or Laurel turning into a jerk and also abandoning me or Sylvester Benjamin-Morgan and being yelled at by a mean lemon-faced publicist! "Anyway, I'm only here for one week! I live in New York! I told you that part already!" I left out the part that I happened to live in the same apartment building as Dr. Maude, because if he knew that, he'd probably say "Then whattya doing wasting my time here—just go knock on her door!"

He shrugged. "Ya want advice? Here's my advice: Watch Dr. Maude on TV. It's a lot more comfortable than those seats they got in there."

Another security guard—equally as big and wide but with a *gun* hanging off his waist—walked up to us. "Is there a problem here?" he demanded.

"No," I squeaked. I already knew Mom and Alan were going to freak about the Sylvester stuff—I did not need to add that I had gotten arrested for stalking Dr. Maude.

"So . . . you going to go get tickets for the shows in two weeks, or what?" asked the first guard.

"No," I sighed. What was the point? I didn't need advice in two weeks—I needed it *now*.

chapter 8

Dear Dr. Maude,

I know that a lot of the time when your guests are telling you their problems on the show, you cut them off and say, "Oh, stop your complaining—just buck up already. This is life, and life is not fair. So deal with it!"

Well, you know what, Dr. Maude? You're right—life ISN'T fair. Because if it were, I'd be doing something FUN—like going to Billy's Bakery with Beatrice, or playing Monopoly with Dad—instead of sitting in Laurel's trailer CRYING because she's being a total jerk. AGAIN. Not only did she get all mad at me for talking to a sleazy tabloid reporter even though I didn't KNOW he was a reporter, but when I finally found my way back to the set after (a) getting lost for a pretty long time and (b) trying to get the security guards to let me into the taping of your show on account of the fact that you and I are friends, she hadn't even noticed I was gone. THAT'S how unimportant I am to her now.

The only good news is that Laurel's publicist Marci was somehow able to convince the sleazy tabloid reporter's boss not to run the article with the stuff I told him (probably because she's totally scary-mean), and Laurel's so busy being a teen superstar that she didn't have time to call Mom and Alan to tell them what I had done. So at least I won't get grounded until I'm back in New York. But still, I can tell that she's REALLY mad. Which totally isn't fair because it's not like I did it on PURPOSE.

My life is so awful at this moment that I'm pretty sure that not even YOU can help me, Dr. Maude.

yours truly,
LUCY B. ParKer

P.S. I keep meaning to tell you—I love the new pics of your dachshunds Id and Ego that you put up on your website. The ones where the three of you are running on the beach? They're sooooo cute.

As I sat in Laurel's trailer blowing my nose into a tissue (thankfully, they were the super-fancy Kleenex Cold Care kind), I realized I had spent more time crying in the past year than all the other eleven years of my life. Except maybe when I was a baby, but I'm not sure because I can't remember that far back. I didn't even care that my eyes were all red and puffy, because I wasn't planning on seeing anyone for the rest of the day. I was even willing to give up lunch, even though Laurel had told me that, like craft services, you could go up for seconds, or even thirds, if you wanted—which just showed how upset I really was. And once we got back to the hotel, I was going to lock myself in the suite and stay there for the rest of the week.

Unfortunately, like all my *other* plans for the week (i.e., having a good time with Laurel), the sitting-alone-being-miserable-in-the-trailer plan was screwed up once there was a knock on the door.

I sniffled, opening the door just a crack. "Sorry, but Laurel's not here. She's on set."

"Oh. Okay. Thanks," said a guy's voice. WAIT—was that ...? I opened the door a tiny bit wider. It WAS. I couldn't believe it—Austin Mackenzie was standing *this-close* to me. Well, it would've been *thatclose* if the door hadn't been there. He started to walk away and then turned back to look at me. Huh. His blond hair was actually a lot more sun-kissed-looking in person than on film, and his blue eyes were super-bright. He was like the male version of Laurel, looks-wise. "Who are you then?" he asked suspiciously. "And what are you doing in her trailer?"

"I'm Lucy B. Parker. I'm her ..." It *definitely* didn't feel like we were fristers anymore. "My mother is marrying her father."

"So you're stepsisters," he said.

"Something like that," I grumbled. Before I could say any more, I spotted Laurel walking toward the trailer. And then stop. And then start making this weird choking noise. Oh no. Please don't let Austin turn around right at that second and see her. Even though I was mad at her for going all Laurel-Moses-superstar on me, after my encounter with Blair, I knew full well how hard it was to be face-to-face with your crush, let alone how hard it must be when it looks like you're choking on a chicken bone and you're squawking like Miss Piggy when she's throwing up a hairball.

Unfortunately, he turned around. I didn't blame him. You'd kind of have to be deaf not to wonder what the noise was. "Are you all right?" he asked Laurel. I wondered if she had been studying Miss Piggy, because she sounded *exactly* like her.

"Yeah"—*squawk*—"I'm—"

"She has really bad allergies," I blurted out. "To, uh . . . the smog in Los Angeles. It's a real problem." I really hoped Laurel appreciated what a good liar I was. I doubted it, though.

"Oh, man—that's awful," he said. Either he was an excellent actor or a really nice person, because he sounded like he genuinely meant it. "Well, I just wanted to come by to introduce myself. I'm Austin Mackenzie," he said, putting his hand out toward her.

I did not understand why super-famous people bothered introducing themselves. It's not like there was a person on the entire planet who didn't know who he or Laurel was, except maybe a few shepherds in Tibet or somewhere like that. By this time she had stopped choking. She put hers out. "I'm..."

The two of us waited for her to say her name, but she just stared at him all scared, like she was going to be crushed by a fax machine come to life like the woman in the movie *Attack of the Killer Office Supplies* that I had seen on cable a couple weeks back. Boy, she got more freaked out about being around her crush than *I* did. Who knew that talking to boys was something I did better than her?

"She's Laurel Moses," I finished. "And she's very happy to meet you." Was I going to have to speak for her like this all week? Maybe if I did that, she'd forgive me for talking to Sylvester. Or at least acknowledge my presence.

"Okay, well, I guess I'll see you on set then," he replied. "I'm looking forward to working with you." At least he didn't say, "I'm looking forward to kissing you," because that would've been kind of obnoxious.

"Um, yeah..." she mumbled.

"She says she's looking forward to meeting you, too," I said, yanking her toward the trailer. "At least that's what she'd say if her smog allergy wasn't doing that thing where it takes away her voice," I said. "See ya!"

I shut the trailer door and turned around to see Laurel sitting on the couch, looking like she had just walked away from a car crash or something. "I can't believe I froze up like that," she said, all dazed.

"Yeah, neither can I," I agreed. Seeing her sitting there, looking more like Laurel-normal-girl and not like Laurel-Moses-teen-superstar, my eyes welled up with tears again. "Laurel, I am SO sorry about what happened with that reporter—" I started to say.

She waved her hand. "Forget about that now. I told you, Marci took care of it. Just don't do anything like that again. Plus, that's nothing compared to the way that I just acted like a total idiot in front of Austin!"

Wow. Were crushes *that* powerful? They could get you to forgive someone for something you were super-upset about only moments before? I shrugged. If she was willing to drop it, so was I. "Laurel, you're going to have to get it together," I said firmly. "Obviously, I don't have any experience with boys, either, but for someone like you, who's performed in front of millions of people at the MTV Awards, I have to believe you can talk to Austin. Even if he is a huge star."

Wait a minute—I was supposed to be mad at her. Why was I being so nice and helping her?

"You're right," she agreed. "I can do this." She stood up and started pacing. "He's just a human being who eats and sleeps and—"

"He probably even farts, too!" I added. I couldn't help it. I was in major-pep-talk-mode. Plus, I didn't want to see her sad, even if she had been being totally mean to me earlier.

"Exactly!" she cried. "I can just go out there and be

normal." She stopped pacing and grabbed my hand. "You know, Sequoia never would've saved me like you did back there," she said. Sequoia was her ex-BFF—the girl who played her BFF on her show, but dumped Laurel because she used too much hand sanitizer and was so organized and weird about it. "I guess I never really knew what it was like to have a best friend before now," she said shyly, squeezing my hand.

Maybe Mom was right about the fact that this teen-age hormone stuff made you totally nuts. I couldn't keep up with Laurel's moods. One minute she was super-mean and the next she was totally my BFF. But I knew that call-ing her on the flip-flopping at this point was not a smart idea. What if she flipped back to being mean?

It sounded stupid, but I still couldn't get over the fact that Laurel thought I was so great. I mean, I was just this normal, untalented, coordination-challenged twelve-and-a-half-year-old, and she was . . . well, Laurel Moses. *Everyone* liked her. Even people who had never met her wanted to be her. Granted, she *was* a little weird. Like with the germ thing. And the neatness thing. And the never-having-been-to-the-mall thing. And about fifty billion other things. But still, despite all the things, every girl in the world would have died to be able to call Laurel her BFF. And she chose . . . *me*, I thought, squeezing her hand back. Even though I said Beatrice was my BFF, the truth was I felt the same way—Laurel *was* my BFF. Well, at least the non-superstar version of Laurel.

There was a knock on the door. "Come in," she yelled out.

A headset-wearing, walkie-talkie-holding production assistant popped her head in. "Laurel, you're wanted on set," she said.

"Thanks," she said. She turned to me. "You ready to go?"

I nodded. I was glad Laurel and I had made up, because the more I thought about it, the more I realized that sitting in a trailer all afternoon by myself would be really boring. Even if there was a TV in there. I'd much rather be with my BFF.

Unfortunately, Laurel missed the part in the BFF manual that said "BFFs don't dump BFFs for boys."

When we first got on set, Austin dragged his chair over to sit next to us (not while the camera was rolling). I still had to help Laurel out with the talking-to-boys stuff for a while. Laurel had no problem memorizing pages and pages of dialogue, but when it came to talking to a boy she liked? Forget it. She just froze up. Sometimes midsentence. Once she actually said, "Excuse me—I have to go to the bathroom. I'll be right back," and ran away, like she had drunk like seventeen large bottles of water. But after a while, we both realized that Austin was a regular human being (and a nice one at that, because instead of ignoring me like I was an annoying little sister, he totally included me in the conversation), and Laurel finally began to relax.

Everything was good until they started playing the "Oh my God—I had no idea you like fill-in-the-blank, too!" game. I HATED that game. Mom and Alan had played it the night we all went to dinner the first time. Back then I had caught Laurel rolling her eyes, but now she sounded just as stupid as Mom and Alan had, and soon enough, I was the one rolling her eyes.

When they first started, I tried to play as well. ("Hey, I like pizza, too!" "I saw that movie, too!") But they both just ignored me. And when you're ignored long enough, you start to feel like a total loser and start picking at your cuticles again, just so you have something to do. I had finally managed to chime in and insert myself into the conversation when both their phones rang at the same time ("Look—we both have phones!") and they had to take their calls ("It's *my* agent on the line, *too*!"). Oh brother.

I thought the morning had gone badly, but this was even worse. Laurel wouldn't even be TALKING to Austin and playing this stupid game if it wasn't for me helping her out! Not only that, but it was like Laurel had taken a pill that had turned her into Cristina Pollock. She flipped her blonde hair around every two seconds, and twisted it around her finger, or giggled at stuff that, frankly, was not funny.

I'd had enough. It was bad enough to be ignored by Laurel-Moses-teen-superstar, but I didn't need to feel like I was back in school and being forced to sit next to Cristina Pollock. I was about to tap her on the shoulder and say, "Laurel? I'm going to go back to the trailer. Not that you care ..." when she turned to me. "Hey, Lucy, Austin and I are going to go to the director's trailer because we have some questions about the scene we're going to shoot later. You'll be okay here without me for a little bit, right?"

Here was my chance to say "Actually, no—I'm feeling sort of left out again, ESPECIALLY since you and I are SUPPOSEDLY BFFs." So I took a deep breath and shrugged and said ... "Whatever," all angry-like.

Now you would THINK that if you were really best friends with a person, then that person would be able to TELL that even though you were saying "Whatever" you definitely didn't mean "Whatever," and that what you REALLY meant was, "How could you ditch me like this after we kind-of, sort-of just made up in your trailer because I totally saved your life with the pep talk I gave you, and the fact that you called me your best friend for the first time!?" But this particular so-called best friend couldn't tell this. Nope—this particular so-called best friend was completely clueless and, instead, just waltzed away in her dumb-looking half-witch costume, leaving the other best friend sitting there yet again by herself, feeling yet again like an idiot.

It was like being friend-dumped all over again. Except instead of being able to avoid the dumper by hiding in the bathroom during lunch, I still had to *live* with her.

chapter 9

Dear Dr. Maude,

I know I've already written you a bunch of e-mails already today, but I'm still in serious need of help. Things with Laurel are really NOT good at the moment. Like they're SO not good that I've almost totally forgotten about trying to figure out if I really do have a crush on Blair, because I'm too busy thinking about how mad I am, and how, the next time Mom and Alan say, "Hey—guess what? We have this really awesome surprise for you: you get to go to L.A. for some bonding time with your soon-to-be frister," I'm going to say, "Thanks, but I think I'd rather spend a week either (a) locked in a room with Marissa, listening to her talk about her doll collection, or (b) walking over hot coals in bare feet."

It's seven at night, and instead of being at dinner with Laurel and Austin, and Murray and Sam, the producers of the movie (BTW—they produced all those comedies about Chopin, the talking cat. Did you ever see them? They were REALLY funny), I'm in the hotel room by myself eating a ham-and-cheese sandwich with balsamic vinegar on top from Urth Caffé. It's not like I wasn't invited to dinner, because I was. But if I learned anything today, it's that there's no way

I'm going to go where I'm not wanted. And believe me—if you saw the way that Laurel was treating me, you would see that I was very much not wanted. And when I said to Laurel, "Actually, I'm really tired, so instead of going to Dan Tana's for dinner with you guys, even though I'm really hungry, because I never ended up finding craft services for lunch, I'm going to just go home," she just said, "Okay. Then I'll see you back there." Not even, "Really, Lucy? You're sure?" or "Hmm . . . that didn't sound very convincing—you're not lying by any chance, are you?"

I don't know who to talk to about this. Unfortunately, I can't call Mom because it's three in the morning in Italy, and after freaking out that I was calling in the middle of the night and thinking there was a real emergency, she'd probably be mad that I woke her up. I tried calling Dad, but he and Sarah were on their way to a "How to Deliver Your New Baby in the Bathtub" lecture. I was right when I said it's totally going to be all about the baby from now on. Plus, he would just say, "Be honest with Laurel about your feelings." But there's absolutely no way I'm doing THAT, because (a) she doesn't deserve it, and (b) she wouldn't listen anyway.

I really hope you get this and e-mail me back with some non-just-be-honest-about-your-feelings advice.

Thanks very much.

yours truly,
LUCY B. PARKER

Hanging out in a hotel room by yourself is really boring. Even if it is the Presidential Suite with a view of the Pacific Ocean and a welcome basket that's so big you've eaten all the chocolate-covered almonds and peanut-butter pretzels and still haven't made a dent in it. Which is why after my sandwich and an hour's worth of *The Real Twelfth Graders of Boston*, I decided to go dip my toes in the ocean.

"Look, Frederick!" boomed a loud voice as I stepped out from the elevator into the lobby. "It's that delightful young girl I was telling you about earlier—the one who eats bread!"

I turned beet red as a roomful of heads swiveled to get a look at the bread eater—i.e., me. Lady Countess Annabel Ashcroft de Winter von Taxi was sitting on the overstuffed couch next to a short bald man and pointing my way.

"It's Lucy, correct?" she went on. "Lucy B. Parker?"

I couldn't believe it. A huge star like Lady Countess Annabel Ashcroft de Winter von Taxi not only remembered my name, but she psychically knew that the "B" part of it was very important to me. I stood up a little taller. "Yes. Yes, it is," I replied.

"Lucy B. Parker, I'd like you to meet my butler-slash-personal-assistant-slash-decorator, Frederick," she said.

"It's nice to meet you," I said, holding out my hand to the bald man.

"*Enchanté*," he said, holding out his. I knew from Beatrice that that meant "enchanted" in French.

"I had no idea you were staying here, too!" she boomed. "What a wonderful little happy accident of fate!"

"You're staying here?" I asked, confused. "I thought you lived in a big house in Beverly Hills with a tennis court and a swimming pool." When you're alone in your hotel room because you've been dumped by your frister, you have a lot of time to Google.

"I do, but I much prefer staying in hotels. Sometimes I go from hotel to hotel, depending on my mood. I just love room service. Now, Lucy B. Parker," she said, grabbing at my hand with her ring- and bangle-covered one, "it's been *forever* since we've seen each other—you *must* tell me everything that's happened since then. I'm just *dying* to catch up." It had been about ten hours. On most regular days if someone asked me that question, I wouldn't have much to report (I had had a mixed-fractions pop quiz? I had stopped at Gray's Papaya on my way home from school for a papaya drink?), but today was not a regular day.

"Why aren't you out with that nice sister of yours? By the way—you were right. She really *is* wonderful. The way she didn't complain in the least as I made the director do seven takes of my close-up!"

Maybe she *used* to be wonderful. But she sure wasn't anymore. "Well . . . it's a long story," I replied.

"Oooh . . . I just *adore* long stories, don't I, Frederick?"

"You do adore long stories, Lady Countess Annabel Ashcroft de Winter von Taxi," he agreed.

"Frederick and I were planning on walking over to the Santa Monica Pier to play a little skee ball," she said. "If you're not busy, perhaps you'd like to join us. The walk over should give us more than enough time to hear the long story."

"You like skee ball?" I asked, amazed. Next to bowling, it was my favorite sport.

"Oh yes—I have a machine in my mansion and everything." She stood up and threw one end of her Indian-looking shawl over the shoulder of her caftan. "Now come on—we'd be just *thrilled* to have you come with us, wouldn't we, Frederick?"

"Yes, Lady Countess Annabel Ashcroft de Winter von Taxi, we would," he agreed, although he didn't sound all that thrilled.

As we made our way out the front door of the hotel, I turned to her. "I completely understand if you say no, but I was wondering . . . Lady Countess Annabel Ashcroft de Winter von Taxi is a real mouthful. So do you think it would be okay if I just called you Lady A?"

From the way Frederick's right eyebrow raised, it wasn't.

"Hmm. No one's ever asked me that before," she said. "When you're royalty—real or just Hollywood—that kind of thing just isn't . . . *done.*"

Great. I had just completely insulted the one person in Hollywood who was talking to me.

"But I love it!" she boomed. "Lady A—that's just *fabulous*!" She turned to Frederick. "Isn't that just fabulous, Frederick?"

"Yes. Just fabulous, madame," he agreed, although it didn't really sound like he thought it was.

"And *you*, Lucy B. Parker, are just fabulous, too!" she boomed.

I tried to give a smile, but it was hard because I sure wasn't feeling fabulous lately. In fact, I was feeling pretty awful. About *everything*.

As we walked down Ocean Avenue to the pier, stopping every block or so so she could sign autographs ("You say your name is Esme? What a *marvelous* name? Lucy and Frederick, isn't that just a *marvelous* name?"), I ended up telling her all about Laurel, and how she had changed when we arrived in L.A., and how I felt like she was dumping me for Austin.

"Oh, to be young again!" Lady A sighed as she threw the skee ball up the ramp. It was a good thing there was a net dividing the ramp from the others, or else the ball would've gone right into their holes. You were actually supposed to roll the ball, not throw it, but apparently no one had told her that part, and I was afraid it might be rude to do so. "The drama! The intrigue! The pathos!

It's just marvelous." She turned to Frederick. "Isn't it just marvelous, Frederick?"

"Yes. Just marvelous," he agreed, standing beside her and holding her cotton candy, caramel corn, and snow cone. He sounded a little less bored than he had been at the hotel, but still bored. When I got back to the suite, I was going to have to look up *pathos*, because I wasn't sure what it meant.

Finally, it was my turn. As I rolled the ball up the ramp, I tried not to get too many points, as I didn't want to hurt Lady A's feelings by beating her. "You wouldn't happen to have any advice for me, would you?" I asked.

"Luckily for you, I absolutely do," she said. "You see, I once had the very same thing happen with *my* sister back when I was around your age."

"You did?" I gasped.

"Oh yes," she said, crunching away on her caramel corn. "Once Martin de Kooning von Helson the Third entered the picture, she dropped me like last year's Louis Vuitton bag. It was just *awful*." She turned to Frederick and grabbed her snow cone from him. "Remember I told you about that, Frederick? Wasn't it just *awful*?"

He nodded. "It did sound quite awful, Lady A."

"And I was at that very tender age of first crushes, and first bras, and many other firsts, so I felt quite abandoned," she said.

"That's exactly how I feel!" I cried. I was so excited to be understood that I forgot that I was trying not to do well and rolled the ball right into the 40 points hole. "So what did you do?"

"Well, I sat her down, and I said, 'Antonia, there's something I need to talk to you about—'"

Uh-oh. I didn't like where this was going. I didn't want to sit down and talk to Laurel. As far as I was concerned, this situation had passed the point of being able to be discussed. "And then what?" I asked warily.

"And then I did a very un-British thing and screamed at her about how mad I was and how hurt and how, as far as I was concerned, she was the world's most horrible sister."

"And then what happened?" I asked.

"Well, she began to cry, and then she said she was sorry, and it was over," she replied.

"That was it? Just like that, it was over?"

She nodded.

"Oh, I don't know if I could do that," I said.

"Why not, darling?" she asked, taking the skee ball from my hand. Frederick and I cringed as she lobbed it in an overhead pitch. Lady A may have had a mantel full of Academy Awards, but she sure wasn't going to be winning any trophies for Best Skee Baller.

"Well, it just seems like the whole thing is past the point of discussing."

"But unless you know for sure that Laurel can read

minds like Kantu, my marvelous psychic who lives in the South of France, you don't know if that's the case," Lady A said.

"Okay, yeah, but also . . . it scares me to fight with people," I admitted. "I mean, with my parents, it's okay, but with friends . . . I don't know. I guess I worry that if we fight, they'll go away forever."

Lady A laughed her trademark combination tinkly-ho-ho-ho laugh. "Oh, darling, fighting is *marvelous*! It means you really care about the person!"

"It does?"

She nodded. "Of course. If you didn't care about the person, you wouldn't bother to fight with her, right?"

I thought about it. "I guess so." I thought about the big fight I had had with Mom when she told me that if she married Alan we'd have to move to New York, and how the only way I had talked to her for the next few days was through Miss Piggy.

"Remember: communication is the key to happy, healthy relationships; and happy, healthy relationships are the key to a happy, healthy heart," she said.

I gasped. That was Dr. Maude's trademark line— the one she ended every show with. "You're a Dr. Maude fan!"

"Oh yes. Frederick and I never miss her show, do we, Frederick?" she asked, grabbing for the candy apple he was holding.

"No, Lady A, we never do," he replied.

Just as I was about to tell her that Dr. Maude and I were neighbors, we were interrupted by a guy's voice: "Hey, is that Lady Countess Annabel Ashcroft de Winter von Taxi?" The three of us turned to see Connor Forrester, Austin's worm-eating BFF, coming toward us. Like Austin, he was actually cuter in person. I mean, if you went for boys who had wavy brown hair the color of caramel and dimples and long eyelashes, which I did not. Or did I? Seeing that I hadn't spent a lot of time thinking about boys and crushes, I had no idea what I went for. "Wow—it is!" he exclaimed.

I felt a weird tingly feeling in my spine when I heard him talk. I wondered if I was getting spinal meningitis, which is this weird disease that I had seen on a program on the Discovery Channel once. I wasn't sure exactly what it was, but it had the word *spinal* in it, so I figured this tingling could be it. But then I realized that weird tingly feeling was the kind of thing that might happen if a person had . . . a *crush*. But I didn't have a crush on Connor Forrester. I had a crush on Blair. And Connor was a superstar. (I mean, yes, I needed to find a celebrity to have a crush on, but it needed to be one who was . . . I don't know, less *cute*. And one who didn't actually eat worms.)

"I'm going by Lady A now," she replied.

"Oh cool. Because that's a real mouthful," Connor said. "*Girls' Guide to Sorcery, Part Four*? You were seriously awesome in that." He stuck out his hand. "I'm

Connor, by the way," he said. Again with the celebrities introducing themselves! He pointed at my giant pretzel. "Hey, would you mind if I tore off a little piece of that?" he asked, not even waiting for a response before he did it. "I'm starved."

Who did this guy think he was? I mean, yes, he was a big movie star; and, yes, every girl I knew had a crush on him. But that didn't mean he could go around interrupting people's conversations and just *taking* their food. And why wasn't that tingly feeling going away? And why did my face suddenly feel all red and hot?

"Hey!" I said. "That's my pretzel. I was eating that."

"Wow. I don't know if I've ever met a girl in L.A. who actually eats bread," he said.

"I said the very same thing!" Lady A boomed.

"Well, that's because I'm not from L.A.," I said. "I'm from New York. And back there, we *do* eat bread." I wanted to add, "At least we don't eat *worms*," but I didn't.

He nodded. "Yeah, I can tell."

My eyes narrowed.

"Hey, I mean it as a compliment. I swear." He squinted. "Wait a minute—I know you! You're the girl who plays the little sister in that show *Laurina's Lessons for Living*."

"What? No, I'm not!" I cried. "I'm Lucy B. Parker!" Why were my palms starting to sweat?

"You know, they really should give you an Emmy for that," he went on. "I myself have never played anyone developmentally disabled like your character is, but I did do a guest role in a very special episode of *Malibu 90265* as a football player suffering from dyslexia, and it was probably the most rewarding acting experience I've ever had."

Okay, I knew he meant it as a compliment, too, but still, having someone think you played a girl with special needs did *not* feel like one. In fact, it felt like an insult. Even though I had seen that show and the girl *was* a good actress. But this was good—it meant that now I *definitely* couldn't have a crush on him. How could you have a crush on someone who insulted you? (Unless, of course, you were Alice. Max Rummel insulted *her* all the time.) "I'm not an actress," I said. "I just happen to live with one." I waited for the oversharing to start, but it didn't. Phew. No oversharing meant that this was *definitely* not a crush then.

"Who?"

"Laurel Moses."

"No way! My best friend Austin's at dinner with her right now!" he said excitedly. His phone buzzed, and he looked at the screen. "Sorry. I have to take this—it's my agent." He looked at me and flashed a smile. "Nice meeting you all," he said. "Bye, Lucy."

I could understand that if you were going to crush on someone, that someone should probably have a really great smile, like Connor did, but it didn't matter how nice his smile was, because I clearly did not have a crush on him. Because if I did, I would've gotten all tongue-tied, like Laurel had around Austin, and obviously that hadn't happened.

"Ta!" trilled Lady A.

I opened my mouth to say good-bye, but nothing came out other than a weird choking noise. Like when Laurel met Austin. Or like when Miss Piggy was about to cough up a hairball.

Uh-oh. This was not good.

chapter 10

Dear Dr. Maude,

I was hoping to find an e-mail from you when I woke up this morning, but no luck. To be honest, I even got out of bed at one in the morning to check because I happened to be awake on account of the whole Connor Forrester thing.

So this is what happened: I was playing skee ball with my new friend Lady Countess Annabel Ashcroft de Winter von Taxi today (Lady A, to her close personal friends such as myself), and Connor Forrester ended up coming up to us. You know who he is, right? That teen actor who does all the movies with monkeys and once ate a live worm? Anyway, I'm a little worried that all of the weird stuff that happened as I was talking to him—like the electrical shocks in my back, and the way that I got tongue-tied— might mean I have a crush on him. But that can't be possible, right? I mean, he's Connor Forrester, a famous star, and I'm just regular old Lucy B. Parker. Yes, every-one's supposed to have a celebrity crush (BTW, do you have one? I'm really good at keeping secrets, so if you tell me, you don't have to worry that I'll blab it), but I think I need one who's not as cute. Or famous.

It's time to leave for set, so I have to go. More later.

yours truly,
Lucy B. Parker

P.S. Any tickets become available by any chance?

P.P.S. Everything is okay between Laurel and me, BTW, so when you write back you can just focus on the advice about what to do when you might possibly have a crush on someone you don't want to have a crush on.

Thankfully, things *were* better with Laurel and me. But before they got better, they had gotten a little worse first.

After Lady A, Frederick, and I got back to the hotel and said good night, I went up to the suite and took out my notebook to make a "Reasons Why I ABSOLUTELY CANNOT Have a Crush on Connor Forrester" list (*1. Beatrice has already chosen him as her celebrity crush. 2. He's way too cute. 3. He's way too famous. 4. He's way too cute*). Then Laurel got back from dinner.

"How was it?" I asked as she bumped into the coffee table because she was looking down at her phone.

"Ow!" She looked up with a goofy smile on her face. "Sorry—did you say something?"

"Yeah. I asked how dinner was." I was so busy worrying about this possible crush situation that I'd almost forgotten that I was still supposed to be mad at Laurel for dumping me, but it was all starting to come back to me.

"Oh, it was just great. Austin is so . . ." She looked back down at her phone and started typing again.

"So what?" I asked.

She looked up with another goofy smile. "Huh? Sorry—did you say something? Austin just sent me the funniest text—"

Okay, that was it. I had had it. I didn't act this way when I got a crush on Blair, did I? And even if I had a crush on Connor—WHICH I DID NOT— but even if I did, there's no way I would ever act like she was acting now. "I did, but it doesn't really matter because ever since we got here you haven't listened to a thing I've said!" I yelled. "It's like from the minute we got off the plane, I don't even know you anymore!" I cried.

"What are you talking about?" she asked, finally looking up from her phone.

"You're just being so . . . *Hollywood*. Like every time I ask you something, I'm bothering you!" I yelled. Boy, when you let yourself get angry, it was pretty hard to stop. "And now you're all Austin this, and Austin that—which, by the way, you wouldn't even be able to *do*, if it hadn't been for me giving you that pep talk and talking FOR you!"

"I—"

I wiped away the tears that had started to come. "I never figured you for the kind of person who would dump someone. Especially her *supposed* best friend."

Now *her* eyes started to fill with tears. "Wait a minute—you think I'm *dumping* you?"

"I don't think it—I know it," I snapped at her, and snuffled. The tears started to fall.

"I would never dump you!" she cried. Her tears started to fall, too. "There's just all this pressure on me right now from my agents and my manager to do all these interviews, and to audition for all these movies that are more dramatic, and then there's Marci, and that whole thing with that skeezy reporter, and I'm kind of freaking out," she admitted.

"How come?"

"Because before I met you I was fine with just focusing on my career, because I didn't really have anything else, you know?" She sniffled. "Not you . . . not a crush. But now that I've met you, I'm getting to do all of these more normal-life-type things . . . I don't know . . . it's really fun. And when you and I hang out together, like during the IBS stuff, I get to be normal. But all this—" she said, motioning to the giant hotel suite, "this is part of my life, too, you know? It's not normal, but it's part of me. And

I guess because I've done it by myself for so long, I keep forgetting that I'm not alone anymore."

I knew exactly what she meant. Like how sometimes I'd reach for the last brownie and take a bite without asking first if she wanted to split it.

"And the whole thing with Austin—I'm really sorry about that, Lucy. You're right—I did get really caught up in the crushiness of it all."

Did? Try "I am." Even though she managed to control herself, I could tell from the way she kept glancing at her phone every time it dinged with a text, she was *still* caught up in it.

"I guess I just got so stuck in the moment." She sighed. "And I guess I just never think of you as the kind of person who ... *needs* someone, I guess."

"What do you mean?" I asked, confused.

"I mean, you're so strong ... and independent ... and able to talk to just about anyone. Everyone loves you. I guess I thought even though I was busy, you'd make all these friends on set."

Again with the strong stuff! What was everyone thinking?! "But I *do* need people," I said. I got all teary again. "Especially you. Do you know how many tissues I've been through since we've been in L.A. because I've been so upset about this?"

"Oh, Lucy—I'm so sorry!" she said, starting to cry harder. "And I need you. Probably even more than you need me. Will you forgive me?"

I wiped away my tears and nodded.

She gave me a big hug. "I love you, frister," I heard her say.

"I love you back," I replied. And I really meant it.

After we unhugged, and Laurel went to go get ready for bed, I reached for my advice notebook.

When you're having a problem with a person, don't be afraid to just tell her the truth about how you're feeling. Because even though it sounds like really dumb advice, it really works, I wrote.

Now that I was officially talking to Laurel again, I told her all about my run-in with Connor Forrester while I got ready for bed. When I was done, she squealed so loud you would've thought she had won an Oscar. "Omigod—I can't believe we have crushes on two best friends! That is *so* cute!"

"Wait a minute—I do *not* have a crush on him," I corrected her.

"Sure you do."

"How can you say that? I said, like, ten words to him." I pretty much remembered every word, so if she gave me a second, I could go over the whole conversation in my head and add it up exactly.

"It's not what you *said*—it's how you *felt*," she replied. "The electrical shocks, the sweaty palms, the not being able to speak." She went to her computer and typed something. A second later she pointed to the screen. At the top it said: "Warning Signs That You Might Have a Crush." "See—they're all right here."

I paled. How did this page not come up when I did my Google search after meeting Blair? This was a disaster! "But I don't *want* to have a crush on Connor Forrester!" I cried. "I want to have a crush on someone who I actually might have a chance with. Like Blair."

"What makes you think you don't have a chance with Connor?" she asked.

"Um, maybe because he's super-famous, and I'm not?" I suggested. "Everyone knows that famous people only like other famous people. Like you and Austin."

"Maybe you're not super-famous, but you're super-fabulous, which is even better than famous," she said. She gasped. "Do you think the four of us can double-date? That would be so cute! Not to mention, the magazines would totally eat it up." She picked up her phone. "Wait till I tell Austin about this," she said, getting ready to text.

"Laurel Moses, if you do that, I will never ever talk to you again!" I yelled, tackling her and yanking the phone out of her hand just in time to see a text ding through. "*You're never going to believe this, but Connor met Lucy... and he thinks she's not bad looking,*" I read aloud.

Laurel squealed.

"'Not bad looking'?!" I cried. "What does *that* mean?"

She squealed again. "It's boy-speak for he has a crush back on you!"

I wondered if "feeling like you're going to throw up" was one of the crush warning signs. For most girls, hearing that Connor Forrester thought they weren't bad looking would be a dream come true, but for me it felt more like a nightmare.

The next night things went from being kind-of-a-nightmare to a full-out-definite-nightmare.

The day part was actually really cool. I went to the set with Laurel again, but when it was time to break for lunch, Lady A asked me if I wanted to go to Beverly Hills with her and Frederick for lunch because she was wrapped for the day (which is what they said in Hollywood when they didn't need her anymore).

"So the gossip blogs aren't lying—you really *do* have a pink car!" I exclaimed as Frederick drove up in what I would soon learn was called a Rolls-Royce.

"Darling, I've never had anything *but* pink cars." She rummaged in her bag and took out a pair of oversize round sunglasses that were identical to hers. "Here— you can wear these. So that we're not mobbed on Rodeo Drive."

"We're going to Rodeo Drive?!" I asked as Frederick opened up the door so we could get in the backseat.

According to Laurel, Rodeo Drive was the fanciest shopping street in all of Beverly Hills, if not all the world.

"Oh yes—it's the only place I shop, isn't it, Frederick?"

"Yes, Lady A," he said, putting on his own oversize sunglasses.

I settled back into the butter-soft leather seat. I had to say, as much as I loved riding the subway in New York, a person sure could get used to this celebrity stuff.

I didn't say this to Lady A, because she liked Rodeo Drive so much, but, frankly, I didn't see what the big deal was. There wasn't an H&M or an Urban Outfitters or Target anywhere on the entire street. There were, however, a lot of older women with the skin of their faces pulled tight who were wearing sunglasses that were just as big as Lady A's and toting tiny yippy dogs. After Lady A did a little shopping, we went to the Peninsula Hotel for high tea. I wasn't big on tea, but I did like the tea sandwiches and cookies that came with it.

"Lady A, can I ask you something?" I said, trying to remember to nibble on my shortbread cookie rather than shove it in my mouth all at once.

"Of course you can, darling," she said. "Anything other than my age."

"Well, see there's this boy—" I started to say.

"The one from last night? The one you seem to have a crush on?"

I turned red. "That's the thing—I don't know if I have a crush on him, because, well"—I felt really stupid admitting this to someone as sophisticated as Lady A—"I've never actually *had* a crush before."

"Really? No local or long-distance ones before this one, the celebrity one?" she asked, surprised.

She knew about the three-crush rule, too? How was that possible? Not only was she old, but she had also grown up in another country. "Nope. But if I did have a crush on Connor—I'm not saying I do, but if I *did*—do you have any advice you could give me about how to act?"

"Oh, but of course I can!" she boomed. "I'm going to let you in on a very important secret, Lucy B. Parker. A bit of advice that has served me well over the years through three husbands, seven almost-husbands, and countless suitors." I scrambled to take out my advice notebook and my purple pen. "I learned this many, many years ago in one of the first movies I did," she went on. "In it, I played a character who, like you, had a mad crush on a boy and spent all her waking hours lovesick and miserable."

Oh no—if I did end up having a crush on Connor, was I going to be *lovesick*?

"And what the script called for me to do, which I then

used in real life as well," she continued, "was to pretend that, instead of letting the boy I was madly in love with *know* I was madly in love with him, I had absolutely no interest in him."

I got as far as the "Pretend to have" part in my notebook when I stopped writing. Sure, maybe Lady A had more experience than I did with boy stuff (anyone did, really), but this pretending thing just didn't feel right to me. "I don't know," I said doubtfully. I mean, it was hard enough just trying to be myself without also having to *not* be myself. The tongue-tiedness would probably come in handy for that, but the idea of trying to be someone I wasn't sounded really tiring. "Pete—he's my doorman—is always saying that you're just supposed to be yourself, whether it's with kids at school, or boys."

"Be yourself?" she asked. "Huh. I wonder what that would be like. I'll have to try it sometime. I've been an actress for so long, I've completely forgotten what being yourself feels like!"

As for me, I had a feeling that even if I wanted to be someone else, I was kind of stuck being Lucy B. Parker forever.

When Lady A and Frederick dropped me off at the hotel (she had decided to stay at the Hotel Bel-Air that night), Laurel was waiting for me in the suite.

"Guess where we're going tonight?" she asked as I walked in.

"On the Haunted Hollywood tour?" I asked excitedly. I had read about it on the plane, and it sounded really cool—they took you to places where famous people had died or hotels that were supposedly haunted.

"Nope. To a cookout in Malibu. On the beach."

"At Howard's house?" I asked. Howard was one of Laurel's agents. I had never met him, but once when I was overlistening, I heard Alan say that Howard's house in Malibu should have a sign in front that said THE HOUSE THAT LAUREL MOSES BUILT because it was built with all the money he made off of her career. Howard always called her "Laurel, babe," which, now that I had been in L.A. for a few days, I realized was a very Hollywood thing to do.

"No. To the house that Austin and Connor rented for the summer!" she replied.

The nauseous feeling came back again. I shook my head. "Uh-uh. No way. I don't want to go to some big party. You go. I'll stay here and watch *The Real Eleventh Graders of Connecticut* preview."

"It's not a big party—it's just going to be the four of us," she said.

That was even worse! That meant that I'd definitely have to talk to him. At least if it was a party-party, I could hide in the bathroom or go drown myself.

"Now go put your bathing suit on."

"Why do you get to decide what we're going to do?" I grumbled.

"Because I'm older—that's why," she said.

I sighed. Fristers. I *knew* she'd end up pulling that at some point.

chapter 11

Dear Dr. Maude,

You're never going to believe where I am—in a car on my way to a barbecue at Austin Mackenzie and Connor Forrester's beach house in Malibu. Which, BTW, I totally don't want to go to, but Laurel's making me because she's older and in charge. Not only that, but I'm wearing one of her bikinis because it turns out I left both my bathing suits at home by mistake. She says it looks really good on me, but I think I look horrible because she's a lot smaller than me on top. Luckily, I'm wearing a sweatshirt and jeans over it, and you can be sure there's NO WAY I'm taking them off, even though it's eighty-five degrees and I'm already sweating.

So if there is any ANY way you can write me back with some advice about how to act in front of Connor, I'd really appreciate it. Lady A says that I should pretend NOT to like him and that'll make him like me more. But Pete, our doorman, is always saying I should just be myself. Needless to say, I'm confused. Especially since I still find it hard to believe that I might have a crush on someone as famous and cute as Connor. He just seems so NOT like the kind of boy I would crush on, you know what I mean?

Oh—one last thing. I was thinking about it, and I realize that in all of these letters, I tend to talk about myself the whole time and never ask you about you. Maybe that's why you never write back. So how are you? Do you have any vacations planned for the summer? Also, you don't have to answer this if you don't want to, but I was wondering if you have a boyfriend.

I look forward to hearing from you.

yours truly,
LUCY B. PARKER

"I thought you said it was just going to be the four of us," I said through gritted teeth as we stood in the doorway of the big wood and glass house on the beach. As a gaggle of itsy-bitsy-teeny-weeny-bikini-wearing mostly blonde teen girls pushed past us to go inside, I hunched over and crossed my arms over my boobs. Even with the sweatshirt on, I was miserable.

"So did I," she said nervously. "My dad's going to *kill* me if he finds out I took you to a big Hollywood party."

I didn't think my mom would be too thrilled about it, either. I was a little nervous, too. I mean, I hadn't even been to a *non*-Hollywood boy-girl party yet. When we finally pushed our way through the crowd, the first thing I saw was Connor on a couch, strumming on a guitar while a whole other gaggle of teen girls (also bikini-wearing, also mostly blonde) said dumb things like, "Oh, Connor, you're *so* talented—you should totally make an album!" and "Oh, Connor—are you just good at *everything* you do?"

"Hey—look who's here!" he said. "It's Laurel Moses and—"

"Lucy B. Parker," I said.

He smiled. "Yeah. I remember your name."

Connor Forrester remembered my name. How was that possible? He turned to the girls. "She eats bread! Isn't that completely rad?"

At the mention of the word *bread* all the girls started buzzing.

"Can we go home now?" I whispered to Laurel. Before she could answer me—hopefully with an "Of course we can, Lucy, because as your big frister, I can understand how uncomfortable you must be at this moment, so why don't we go back to the hotel and order a pizza and stuff ourselves as we watch something on pay-per-view?"—Austin walked in from the deck. I watched as they did that their-eyes-met-across-a-crowded-room thing that always happened on the *telenovelas* that I liked to watch with our housekeeper, Rose. "Hey, Laurel," he said, all dreamy-like, when he was standing in front of us.

"Hi, Austin," she replied, her eyes now so googly that you could barely see the blue part because her pupils were so big. When I went online before we left, I saw that the gossip blogs were already calling them Laustin.

"Hey, Lucy," he said, not bothering to take his eyes off Laurel.

"Hi," I said glumly.

"Sorry about the crowd," he said. "You know how these things get—you mention to one person that you're having a little barbecue and before you know it, half the city finds out."

Actually, I didn't know anything about how these things got, seeing that I was just a normal twelve-and-a-half-year-old girl and he was a ginormous fourteen-year-old superstar. "There are grown-ups here, right? Like your mom, right? Because my dad and her mom would kill me if they knew I had taken her to a party where there weren't any adults," she babbled.

"Yup—my mom's in her room watching a movie. Want to meet her?" he asked.

"Meet your mom? Now?!" she asked nervously. "Um, maybe later."

He shrugged and smiled at her. "Hey, wanna see the beach?"

She turned to me. "Are you going to be okay if I leave you alone for five minutes?"

I shrugged. "I guess so." As long as I found the bathroom I would be. Or a cookie.

She pulled me aside. "Try not to talk to anyone too old, okay?" she ordered.

I rolled my eyes. "Yes." Boy, she was going to be a really annoying mother when she grew up.

After they walked away, I turned back and scanned the room for snacks. Connor was still strumming away on the couch, and he said, "So how you doing, Lucy B. Parker?"

I opened my mouth, but nothing came out. Oh no. Not the tongue-tied thing again. I cleared my throat. "I ... um ... I ... " I started to say. Then I sprinted toward the kitchen.

As I passed the front door it opened, and another group of kids barreled through—not one sweatshirt in the bunch. I realized it was going to be a long night. I felt like Alice when she drank the potion that said "Drink Me" and fell down the rabbit hole. Not only did I feel small, but it was like my potion also made me feel invisible. Here I was, at my first boy-girl party ever, and half the people were super-famous and all over TV and movies. But instead of being excited about that, or the fact that I was in the same house as a boy whom I may or may not have had a crush on, all I could think about was how I would've much rather been playing Monopoly with my dad in Northampton or hanging out on the couch in the lobby of my apartment building listening to Pete go on and on about what he'd do if he were president.

Luckily, because I was in a house where two boys lived, the kitchen was stocked with all sorts of very un-L.A.-like bread-and-sugar-based snacks that helped to make me feel a little better and a little less lonely. As did the text from Laurel saying "R U OK?"

Until a trio of Bikini Butts wandered in.

"Omigod—is that an *Oreo*?" one of the girls asked.

I couldn't talk because my mouth was full of them, so I just nodded.

"I had no idea they even made those anymore," another of the girls said.

I held the package out. "Want one?" I asked after I swallowed. Food was a good way to make friends.

They all shook their heads in unison. "You're not from here, are you?" asked the third one.

"Nope. I'm from New York City," I said proudly. From the looks on their faces, you'd think I'd said I was from Mars instead of New York. Uh-oh, I could feel the oversharing coming on. "Technically, I'm not a native ... I'm originally from Northampton, Massachusetts ... but Pete—he's my doorman—says that even though I've lived there only a few months, I totally have the personality of someone who was born there. But how'd you know I wasn't from here?" I asked.

"Because no one in L.A. eats Oreos," the first one explained. "We eat Pinkberry."

"Right," I said. "No Oreos, no bread, no walking ..."

A fresh wave of confused looks came over their faces. "Huh?" said the second one.

"What are you doing at this party anyway?" another one of the girls asked. "You're, like ... really young."

Yes, that was true, and, yes, I was feeling it, big-time, but still, she was so rude to say that to me! "I am not really young," I said defensively. "I'm twelve and a half."

"Yeah, but what are you *doing* here?" asked another one.

I sighed. These girls were going to end up having really bad karma if they kept acting like this. I didn't like what I was about to do, but I had no choice. "I'm here because Laurel Moses is my frister," I replied. I almost added, "And because Connor Forrester asked that I come here," but thankfully I didn't. Because even though no one would be able to blame me for oversharing on account of the fact that being questioned by a bunch of older Bikini Butts makes a person really nervous, I had a feeling saying something like that would *not* be good.

At that, their eyes got all wide. They looked like dolls.

Another text came through. *How come ur not answering me? R U OK? Do u need me to come get u???* I grabbed the entire pack of Oreos for the road. Now that I knew no one in the state of California was going to eat them, I didn't feel so bad taking them. "And if you'll excuse me, I'm going to go find her."

As I walked out into the living room, the crowd seemed to have doubled, which made it hard to get toward the glass door to go out toward the beach. I couldn't see Laurel, or Austin, or even Connor. So instead of pushing through all the strangers, I decided just to head for the bathroom and lock myself in there. It was total déjà vu of how I spent my first lunch period at my new school—especially when I started crying. Unfortunately, because it was a boys' bathroom, they didn't have any good tissues, and there was hardly any toilet paper around, so I just used the sleeve of my sweatshirt to wipe my tears. But when you're stuck in a bathroom crying, it gets pretty hot, so finally I just took it off.

I stared at myself in the mirror, and Pete's voice popped into my head. *All you gotta do is be yourself. If you do that, you can't go wrong.* "Okay, Lucy," I said out loud. "You're going to go out there, and you're going to walk over to someone, and you're going to say, 'Hi. I'm Lucy B. Parker. What's your name, and why don't you tell me about yourself?'" One of the things I had noticed about L.A. was that people loved to talk about themselves—even more so than in New York—so even if it didn't make me any new friends, it would at least take up a lot of time while I waited for Laurel to say we could leave. "And after that, you're going to ..."

I was stumped. What *was* I going to do after that?

Before I could figure it out, there was a loud sound from over near the bathtub, followed by a huge crash and a moan.

"*Ooof.*"

I yanked back the shower curtain to find Connor Forrester splayed out in the tub with his eyes closed, holding his head. "Ahhh!" I screamed.

"That window is *small*," he announced. "How's a person supposed to climb in through there without killing himself?" He opened his eyes. "Oh, hey—it's . . . *you*." He turned red and gave a nervous laugh. "Jeez, I'm *really* embarrassed now."

Connor Forrester got embarrassed, too? Who knew?

"Hey, I was wondering—for some reason I was thinking about this yesterday during the photo shoot I did for *Seventeen*—do you think a person could actually die of embarrassment? Not, like, metaphorically, or whatever that word is, but *literally*?"

How many hours had I spent wondering that exact same thing? The tingly feeling in my spine started coming back, and when I looked down, I realized I was probably about to find out if you really could die of embarrassment for sure. Because in all the excitement of having someone break into the bathroom I was hiding in, I had completely forgotten I had taken my sweatshirt off and was standing there in my teensy-weensy bikini top. My body may have been pale, but at that moment, my face sure wasn't. In fact, if it was as red as it felt, I'm sure I looked like a tomato. I quickly reached for my sweatshirt. I wished I could hide behind something. The minute I got out of this bathroom, I was going to have to go drown myself in the ocean.

"And why are you climbing through windows?" I demanded, wiping my sweaty palms on my jeans. A thought flashed through my head—what if I'd been *peeing* when he climbed in?!

"Oh. 'Cause of the girls," he sighed. "There was a whole group of them coming toward me, and it was the only way I could get away. I learned that move in the film *Goin' Bananas* that Austin and I did with that chimp." He shuddered. "Man, was he a pain in the butt. Whenever it was time for someone else's close-up, he totally freaked out."

"Austin?" I asked.

He rubbed his head. "No—the chimp."

Even with my sweatshirt on, I crossed my arms in front of my chest. "Look, I know this is your house and all, so you can do what you want," I said. "But it's kind of rude to just jump in windows without knocking or anything. People go into bathrooms because they want *privacy*." So they can cry. Or hide from Bikini Butts. Or from boys they may or may not have had a crush on. Another text came through. *Lucy, where r u??? I'm freaking out!* I sighed. She was going to explode if I didn't respond. *I'm fine. I'm just in the bathroom,* I typed. I wasn't fine, but the last thing I needed was Laurel coming over and making the whole thing even more embarrassing.

"I know," he said. "Sorry 'bout that. Hey, when you're done in here, you want to go for a walk on the beach or something? The sunset is completely rad."

Connor Forrester had just asked me to go on the beach with him. At sunset. That seemed like something you'd ask a person that you kind-of, sort-of didn't hate to do with you. If I said yes, it would be a good opportunity to see if I really did have a crush on him. But then there was always the chance that I would embarrass myself in ways I couldn't even imagine, and this trip had already been eventful enough without having to deal with *that*. "Thanks, but I can't," I said nervously. "I, uh . . . I'm not allowed to be outdoors at sunset time."

"How come?"

"I have a rare skin disease," I replied.

"You do?" He squinted. "You're kind of pale, but you look okay to me."

"That's because it only kicks in if I'm out at sunset." I was getting really good at coming up with realistic lies on the spot.

"Okay," he shrugged, opening the door to leave. "See you around then, I guess."

"Yeah. See you around," I replied as I watched him walk through the door.

I was probably the only girl in America who would choose to stay locked in a bathroom rather than walk on the beach with Connor Forrester.

Was "completely losing your mind" another warning sign of a crush? I made a mental note to look that up when we got back home.

chapter 12

Dear Dr. Maude,

Boy, this iTouch really has come in handy, huh? If I didn't have it, I wouldn't be able to e-mail you all the time. Okay, you are NEVER going to believe what just happened to me. So this BBQ at Austin and Connor's has turned into a full-blown boy-girl party, which is why I'm hiding in the bathroom, and who do you think just came flying through the window? You probably won't guess, so I'll tell you—CONNOR FORRESTER.

Thankfully, I wasn't, you know, peeing or anything embarrassing like that—I was just talking to myself in front of the mirror—but still, it was awkward. Especially because I was wearing just a bikini top. I mean, that's not ALL I was wearing—I was wearing my jeans, too—but . . . anyway, that part's not important. What's important is the fact that Connor asked me if I wanted to go for a walk on the beach because it's supposedly a rad sunset.

Now, I don't have a lot of experience with boys—okay, I don't have ANY experience with boys—but still I've seen enough movies to know that walking on the beach at sunset is a very romantic thing to do. In fact, when Mom's BFF

Deanna made her sign up for SoulMates.com so she could meet a guy (this was obviously before she met Alan), I snuck a look at Mom's profile, and she had listed "walks on the beach at sunset" in the Romantic Things I Like to Do section, which was news to me. So was the fact that she weighed 125 pounds, because once when I was looking over her shoulder as she got on the scale it said 132, but I didn't say anything, because I was kind-of, sort-of technically snooping.

I'm not sure what advice I'm asking for here because I already told him I couldn't go, but I just thought you'd want to know that. Plus, typing this gave me something to do while I'm trying to avoid going back out into the party.

yours truly,
Lucy B. Parker

P.S. I don't mean to be a pain, but any news on tickets for the show?

I'm not really a claustrophobic person, but forty-five minutes in a bathroom is a long time, even if you're taking a bath, and the last thing I wanted was for people to think I had stomach problems or something gross like that. When I walked back out into the living room, there were now even more Bikini Butts all over the place. And not only that, but even more famous people had arrived, including this guy Clayton Carr, who had just played the totally average, no-special-powers son of two superheroes in this movie that was playing near our apartment back home. What was I, Lucy B. Parker—so unpopular that she was still known as the New Girl at school (or Period Girl, ugh!)—doing at a party with the most popular kids in the entire universe? And not only that, but they were all like two years older than me.

Which is why it totally made sense that I then sprinted outside onto the deck. At least it was quiet out here, with just the sound of the waves. And like Connor said, the sunset *was* super-pretty.

I looked around for Laurel and Austin, but there was no one else around, and because I was near the ocean, I didn't have reception on my phone to text her. Rolling up the legs of my jeans, I started walking on the beach. I knew it was littering, but because of my poor sense of direction, every few steps I threw part of an Oreo down to leave a trail so I wouldn't get lost. In the distance, I saw a guy who kept whipping around holding an imaginary gun like he was a character in an action-adventure movie. At least he looked like he was enjoying himself, unlike me, who had tears falling down her cheeks—again!—because she felt like an idiot for spending her time hiding in bathrooms and not being able to talk to boys or strangers or anything.

Just then the crazy guy stopped trying to shoot the bad guys, put down his imaginary gun, and started

waving at me. At first I assumed he thought I was someone else. But when I looked around, I realized I was the
only one on the beach, and I got scared. I wasn't going to
die from embarrassment—I was going to die because I
was alone on the beach with a crazy person, and no one
was around to hear me scream if he attacked me.

Crazy Guy stopped waving at me and started jogging
toward me. I turned around and started sprinting away
from him. But because of the sand and my coordination
problem, I couldn't go very fast.

"Lucy!" I heard the Crazy Guy say. "Wait up a sec!"

Oh my God—how'd he know my name? Maybe he
was some freak who was stalking Laurel, and he was
planning on kidnapping me and holding me hostage
until she agreed to go out with him. I huffed and puffed
my way through the sand, cursing myself for skipping so
many gym classes. As soon as I got back to New York—if
I *did* get back to New York—I was going to take up jogging. But when I tripped and landed flat on my face, it
looked like I was doomed.

"You decided to come for that walk!" I heard Crazy
Guy say as I sat up and wiped the sand off my face. When
I managed to get it out of my eyes, I realized that Crazy
Guy equaled Connor.

"What? Oh, yeah," I said, trying to sound all noncha-
lant. "And now I'm just, you know, sitting here taking a
little break. Enjoying the view. Boy, you were right—the
sunset sure is pretty tonight," I babbled.

His eyes narrowed. "But what about that rare skin disease thing?"

"Oh, it's okay," I replied. "I just have to be careful at the *beginning* of the sunset. Once it gets to the middle or end, I'm safe."

"Well, do you want to, I don't know . . . walk for a while?" he asked.

"With you?" I replied nervously.

He shrugged. "Yeah. I mean, we don't *have* to . . ."

"No, it's okay. I guess I could do that."

"Cool." He held his hand out.

"What are you doing?" I asked, confused.

"Helping you up."

"Oh." I reached for it. I don't know what I expected a boy's hand to feel like, but I didn't think it would be so . . . *soft*. Or mushy. It wasn't mushy in a *bad* way, though. It actually felt kind of nice. Like the bagels from H&H.

As we started walking, he started talking. And talking. And talking. It wasn't *like* he told me his whole life story—he *did* tell me his whole life story, starting with how he was almost born in a taxicab in Chicago. Usually, I found those people who went on and on about anything and everything like their favorite cereal and what they thought happened when you died really annoying (hello, Marissa and Alice), but in this case I was glad just to listen. It gave me time to try to figure out how to make my legs stop feeling like Jell-O and how to get my tongue moving again so that in case he asked me a question, I could answer it.

Just then he stopped walking and turned to me. "Hey, Lucy?" he said, his hand moving toward my cheek.

"What are you doing?" I demanded. Was he going to kiss me? He couldn't do that! I wasn't even sure I for sure had a crush on him yet!

"I was just going to tell you that you had a piece of seaweed on your face from when you wiped out back there," he said.

"Oh," I said as I felt my face get hot.

"Dude, it is *so* cool how your face gets red so fast," he said. "When Austin and I did that movie *Chimp Island*—the one with the killer chimps?—there was this special effect where, whenever one of the mechanical chimps bit us, it made our entire bodies turn *green*. It was gnarly."

Before I could say, "That's kind of disgusting," his hand touched my cheek, and that's when it happened.

Not a kiss, but the blinding flash of a camera right in our faces.

"Ha! Gotcha, Forrester!" a safari-jacket-wearing guy yelled over his shoulder as he ran back toward the road.

I couldn't believe it—a "pap" had just snapped a picture of Connor Forrester and me! This was not good. In fact, my psychicness told me it might be very, very bad.

"Man, I can't believe Vinnie Vincenza finally got me!" Connor said, stomping his foot.

"That was Vinnie Vincenza?" I asked nervously. Laurel had warned me about him. His pictures were the ones that ended up in the really sleazy gossip magazines. I didn't even want to *think* about what kind of lie they were going to make up if they ran this one. One time, back in Northampton, a pap took a picture of Laurel, Alan, Mom, and me where it looked like I was picking my nose, when really I was just trying to hide the huge pimple on the side of my face.

"Yeah," Connor said. "I wonder if he thought you were the special-needs sister from that TV show."

Great. "Well, I should get back," I said. Now a fluttering in my stomach had joined the electric shocks. This was getting really annoying.

"Oh yeah?" he said, disappointed.

"Yeah. Laurel's probably worried about me," I said, smacking my stomach to try to get the fluttering to stop.

Forget Laurel—*I* was worried about me. All of these crush symptoms were getting worse, and I wasn't sure how much more I could take.

chapter 13

Dear Dr. Maude,

I hope you don't think I'm being rude for saying this, but I just want you to know that I really think if your viewers knew about everything that had happened to me in the last few months and found out that you had the opportunity to have me on your show, but didn't, they would be VERY upset. ESPECIALLY if they found out that tonight I ended up hanging out with Connor Forrester. By myself. Just him and me. On the beach. At sunset. But it wasn't a date.

Except even though it wasn't a date, how come I keep thinking about him and can't fall asleep? Which is why I'm writing this to you at two o'clock in the morning. Laurel says the reason I keep thinking about him is because I like-like him, and I just haven't admitted it to myself, but I think she's wrong. Like I said, Connor Forrester + me = CRAZY. Plus, when she said that she was half sleeping because I had gone into her room and said, "Laurel? Are you sleeping? Because if you're not, I have a question for you," really loud, and even though she said, "No. I'm up. What's wrong?" her voice was all froggy, which means that she was sleeping. And everyone knows that most of what people say when they're sleeping doesn't mean anything.

I don't know if the world was such a confusing place back when you were twelve and a half, but I'm telling you—you would NOT want to be a kid nowadays!

yours truly,
Lucy B. parker

When you don't fall asleep until three o'clock in the morning, being woken up at eight by your frister, saying, "Lucy, Lucy—you have to get up," is bad enough— especially when she's a total morning person and you're totally not. But when that frister is also shoving a laptop in your face and saying, "You have to see this *now*!" it's worse. Especially when she manages to wrestle the covers away from your head so you HAVE to open your eyes.

"AHHHHHH!" I shrieked when I got a look at what "this" was. Smack in the middle of HottGossip.com was the picture of Connor and me on the beach with a huge headline: "Romantic Sunset + New Gal Pal = Time to Smooch!" Underneath the picture it read, "Looks like teen heartthrob Connor Forrester is following in BFF Austin Mackenzie's footsteps. While sources tell us that Austin and costar Laurel Moses were taking their on-screen romance offscreen last night at the boys' beachfront bash, Connor was getting to know Laurel's soon-to-be little sister Lisa just a little bit better during a romantic walk on the beach."

"Oh no!" I cried. I didn't know what was worse—that they had printed the picture, or that they had gotten my name wrong.

"I hate to be the one to tell you this," Laurel said, "but this picture definitely looks like two people who like-like each other." She squinted as she looked at the picture. "What's that on your face?"

"Seaweed," I moaned, pulling the covers back over my head. This was just awful. I pulled them back down. "Maybe no one will see it," I said hopefully. "I mean, HottGossip isn't *that* popular."

Laurel pointed to the #1 GOSSIP SITE ON THE WEB! line, which was written in big bold letters across the top. "And I hate to tell you this, but it's on at least ten other sites. Probably more, but I stopped counting after that."

I scooched deeper underneath the covers. If the thing about Connor and me were true, maybe I could've dealt with it, but when I got back to New York and seventh grade started and kids came up to me and said, "I can't believe you dated Connor Forrester—what was it like?" and then I'd have to say, "Um, actually, I didn't. That was just something they made up," and then they'd say, "Oh. Well, see you around," then I'd feel even *more* stupid.

I grabbed my iTouch and looked at my mailbox. There were three e-mails from Beatrice, four from Alice, and nine from Marissa, all essentially saying the same thing: "I CAN'T BELIEVE YOU KISSED CONNOR FORRESTER!!!! HOW COME YOU DIDN'T TELL ME????" I'd have to deal with that later. It was a good thing Mom and Dad and Alan didn't go on those sites or else I'd REALLY have trouble. "What am I going to do?" I wailed.

Laurel shrugged. "You just hold your head high, and if a reporter stops you, you say, 'No comment.' That's what I do."

"No reporter is going to stop me," I scoffed. "I'm not a big star like you or Connor." I was just a normal kid. They couldn't even get my name right. No one cared what I had to say most of the time anyway, so why would they start caring now?

When we got down to the lobby, there were about ten or so reporters and photographers camped out there.

"Laurel! Laurel!" a bunch of them yelled as we got out of the elevator and a fireworks-like explosion of flashes went off in our faces. "Are you really dating Austin Mackenzie?"

She put on her sunglasses. "No comment," she said as she began to make her way toward the exit.

Phew, I thought as I put my fancy new sunglasses on and started to follow her. I knew I was right in thinking that they'd care only about Laurel. I was already yesterday's news. Literally.

"Lisa! Lisa!" a few more of them yelled. "What's it like to kiss Connor Forrester?"

Uh-oh. Maybe not. As another round of flashes went off, I was momentarily blinded and ended up tripping, which, in turn, set off *another* round of flashes. When I got back on my feet, I took off my sunglasses and turned to the reporters. "Okay, my comment on that is no comment," I announced. "But before I don't comment, I just want to say that (a) my name is not Lisa—it's Lucy. Lucy B. Parker." I watched as a few of the reporters whipped out their pens and pads. "That's P-A-R-K-E-R, if you end up putting it in an article, but to be honest, I'd really rather you didn't. And (b) I did not kiss Connor Forrester. *I repeat*—I. Did. Not. Kiss. Connor. Forrester."

Uh-oh. That was a lot of no-commenting for someone who didn't have any comment.

"*Sure* you didn't," a guy with Brillo-pad hair said. "So what was it like?"

I rolled my eyes. "I just told you—I didn't kiss him! In fact, not that it's any of your business, but I've never kissed anyone. Ever." A few of them started scribbling away. Oh NO! *Why* did I have to pick that moment to overshare?! "Please don't write *that* part down," I said.

"So are you madly in love?" asked a woman who was so tan she looked orange.

"What do you have to say about the fact that before you, every girl he's been seen with is tall and blonde and you're so . . . *not* tall and blonde?" asked a guy with a T-shirt that said WILL WORK FOR FAME.

"Okay, (c) I am not in love with him, and (d) I happen to like my hair now that it's grown out after I burned most of it off a while back." I put my sunglasses back on. "Now, if you'll excuse me, I have no more comment on the matter," I said as I marched toward the exit.

Laurel said that because Lady A kept forgetting her lines the day before—and then couldn't read the cue cards because she didn't like to wear glasses in front of people—the movie was behind schedule, which meant that she didn't have to work that day. Which meant that we could finally have a frister-to-frister non-Austin-involved sightseeing-slash-bonding day.

"Are we going on the Haunted Hollywood tour?" I asked excitedly as we had breakfast at this place called John O'Groats, which had the best blueberry pancakes and biscuits I had ever tasted in my life. The biscuits were so good that after eating Laurel's, I asked the waitress if I could have another one, which made her say, "Jiminy Crickets—finally someone who eats bread in this country!" in her Irish accent.

"No, we're going shopping . . ." Laurel said.

Shopping? Ugh. We could do that in New York. Plus, I'd just gone shopping with Lady A. I was hoping we were going to do something you could only do out here. But NOT something in the getting-your-picture-snapped-on-the-beach-in-Malibu-by-a-pap family.

"Shopping for something to wear to the *Fifteen Candles* premiere!" she added.

"Are you serious?" I squealed. *Fourteen Candles* had been my favorite movie of last year, and this was the sequel.

She nodded. "It was hard to get on the list," Laurel said. "I had to promise I'd tape a special 'Congratulations on your Bat Mitzvah' message for the head of the studio's daughter, but I know how you've been dying to see it."

"So it's just you and me?"

She nodded. "It'll be our IBS outing for the week."

This was amazing. This almost made up for the really horrible first part of the week. If only the girl who was staring right at Laurel would stop. It was kind of freaking me out. I shifted in my seat so I didn't have to look right at her. Granted, maybe because we were in L.A. and they were more used to seeing famous people, not as many came up and interrupted our meals, but still, having someone watch you while you ate was really annoying, because it meant you couldn't just scarf it all down.

A minute later there was a tap on my shoulder. I turned around. "It *is* you!" she gasped.

"Huh?" What was she talking about?

"You're Lisa—the girl who was kissing Connor Forrester on the beach last night!" she squealed.

Laurel and I looked at each other, alarmed. She wasn't supposed to be interrupting our meal to talk to *me*—she was supposed to be talking to *Laurel*. The girl grabbed my arm. "He's so cute. I *have* to know—is he a good kisser? I know I'm a lot older than him, but he's just to die for."

I yanked it back. "Okay, (a) it's Lucy—not Lisa, and (b) I don't know because I DIDN'T KISS HIM!" I cried. "We're just friends, I swear."

"I can't believe I'm standing right in front of some-one whose lips touched Connor Forrester's," she went on. She whipped out her phone and started texting. "Can I take a picture? My friends are totally going to die when they find out."

I looked at Laurel, alarmed. What was going on? *I* wasn't the one people were supposed to make a big deal about—*she* was.

By the time we were done browsing in the shops on Third Street in West Hollywood, Laurel had been stopped for her autograph three times. And me . . . *four*.

"Wow. I don't think I've ever been with anyone more famous than I am," she said as we walked back to the car. "It's kind of weird."

"And I've never been famous," I said. I shielded my face as a trio of Japanese tourists snapped away at me. "It's *definitely* weird."

A few minutes later the car pulled into the parking lot of a store with a sign outside of it that said Frank Pigeon. I knew before we even went inside that it was really fancy on account of the cars outside. There wasn't one dinged-up Volvo in the lot (which was the kind of car that Mom had had when we lived in Northampton). They were all shiny black Mercedes and BMWs, which I knew from overlistening to Dad were what "greedy capitalists" drove. I wasn't sure what a capitalist was, but I could tell from the tone of his voice that it wasn't good.

The other reason I knew it was a much nicer store than H&M or Urban Outfitters was because when we walked inside and passed a rack of T-shirts that were all faded—like someone had put bleach in the washing machine—I glanced at the price tag on one.

"They want someone to pay a hundred and twenty-five dollars for this?!" I yelled. This place was as bad as those stores on Rodeo Drive.

"Shh," Laurel said, turning red and pulling her hat down a little farther on her head.

An Asian girl wearing the same T-shirt but in red came walking over to us. She looked like one of the Bikini Butts from the night before, except not blonde. "Excuse me, but can I help you?" she asked, all snotty. Was there something in the water that made people in L.A. so stuck up? Because they sure weren't like this back in New York.

Laurel flashed a smile. "No, we're just looking."

"Well, I'm going to have to ask you to keep your voices down," she said. Had I missed the sign that said this place was a *library*? The girl squinted. "Wait a minute—you're Laurel Moses."

Laurel nodded. Okay, this was better. This was the way it was *supposed* to be—Laurel being noticed and me fading into the woodwork. Sure, I may have complained about it in the past (or, like, two days ago), but now I realized it wasn't so bad.

"Cool," she said as if she barely cared. When you thought about it, celebrities were some of the only people who could afford to buy $125 bleach-stained T-shirts, so the salespeople here were probably used to seeing them all the time. She turned to me, and her eyes widened. I got nervous. Was I going to get thrown out because I wasn't famous? Because instead of being a Somebody-with-a-capital-S, I was a nobody-with-a-little-n?

"You're the girl who kissed Connor Forrester on the beach last night!" she announced in a very non-library-like voice. She grabbed my arm. "Omigod—you guys make *such* a cute couple! Are you looking for something special? Maybe something for a date with Connor?" Suddenly, she couldn't have been friendlier. It was like how the kids at school treated me once they found out I was living with Laurel.

"What?! No!" I cried.

"It's for the premiere of *Fifteen Candles*," explained Laurel.

The salesgirl *click-clacked* over to a rack. "I have the perfect thing." Uh-oh. I'd seen what L.A. people wore to premieres on the gossip blogs, and there were some pretty crazy outfits.

When she turned around, she was holding a purple maxidress with pink and red flowers splashed all over it. It was beautiful. And purple. It was PERFECT. I was so grateful for her good taste, it almost made up for the fact that I totally saw that she stopped to Tweet about Connor Forrester's new girlfriend being there.

"It's beautiful," I said. "And not only that, but I bet it'll make my boobs look smaller!" I announced, as I went into the dressing room.

"We're so getting that for you," Laurel said as soon as I walked out of the dressing room. Unlike some people (say, Cristina Pollock), I don't walk around thinking I'm a supermodel, but in this case, the salesgirl was right—the dress *did* look great on me. And I was right, too—it *did* make my boobs look smaller.

"Try these on," the salesgirl said, handing me a pair of gold sandals.

They were pretty, but . . . "But these have . . . *heels*," I said, alarmed. "And if this is a premiere and I'm with you, that means I'm going to have to walk down the red carpet. With photographers!" Sure, I wanted to see the movie, but suddenly this didn't seem like such a good idea.

"They're not heels-heels," said Laurel. "They're what

are called kitten heels. They're totally easy to walk in. I swear."

I gave her a doubtful look. "Yeah, maybe for someone who doesn't have a coordination problem."

"Just try them," she said.

I put them on and clomped across the room as Laurel and the salesgirl cringed. "Huh. They're not so bad," I admitted. I took another step, twisted my ankle, and almost went down.

"We'll work on the walking part later." Laurel sighed.

"You're going to look *so* cute in the pictures they take of you and Connor tonight!" the salesgirl squealed.

I rolled my eyes. "No, I'm not," I replied. "Because there aren't going to *be* any pictures of Connor and me, because Connor's not going. I'm going with Laurel."

Laurel looked up from her phone. "Actually . . . he is," she said. "Austin just texted me, and said he was able to get two tickets, too . . . after he promised his agent he would come to his son's Career Day at school. So he's bringing Connor."

My eyes narrowed. "Did you plan this?" I asked suspiciously.

"No!" she said. "Lucy, you're not the only one who wants to see *Fifteen Candles*. I mean, the first one *was* the number one movie at the box office for forty weeks."

"I guess," I said.

"Omigod—two sisters going on a double date with

two best friends?" the salesgirl piped up. "That is just the *cutest!*"

"I know—right?" agreed Laurel.

"Wait a minute—this is *not* a double date," I corrected her. "It's just four people who happen to be going to the same movie. And *might* sit next to each other." Even if I had been sure I had a crush on Connor—which I *wasn't*—but even if I had been, having a crush was way different than going out on a date! You needed days to prepare for a date. Maybe even weeks. Not to mention that I was only twelve and a half—I highly doubted even Cristina Pollock had gone out on an actual date yet. You were supposed to have crushes first, and ease into it, not skip right to a maybe-date! "Plus, in order for it to be a real date, you have to share popcorn, and I am *not* doing that with him," I added. "His hands have touched *worms.*"

Laurel pushed me back into the dressing room. "Okay, you don't have to share your popcorn, but you do have to take the dress off so we can get going. Roger and Maya are going to do our hair and makeup. We still have a lot to do to get ready for our big da—"

"Don't even *think* about saying what you're about to say," I warned.

"—night at the movies," she finished.

A night at the movies that was just going to happen to include walking down a red carpet in heels while the paparazzi blinded me with flashes and I tried not to break my neck with each step. That was a little different than when Dad used to take me to the Northampton Quad Cinema, where you had to look at your seat before you sat down to make sure there wasn't gum stuck to it.

Another thing that a night at the movies in Northampton didn't include was a trip to the Olympic Spa where, after sweating in a steam room, stocky Korean women in black bikinis scrubbed all the dead skin off your body with this scratchy, sponge-looking thing. While you lay on a table *naked*, with your eyes squeezed shut because you were completely mortified, even though, according to Laurel, the Korean women could care less because they had seen a gazillion naked bodies before.

"Okay, just so I understand right—this is supposed to be *fun*?" I yelled over to the next table where Laurel was also being scrubbed. Unlike my table, there were no "Ooh! Ouch!" sounds coming from it.

"Yeah," she yelled back. "It was listed in *InBeauty* as one of the best places to go before a da—a night at the movies. Isn't it great?" she asked, all excited.

"Actually, it's more like really painful!" I yelled back.

"You'll see—your skin is going to be so soft when they're done," she went on.

The Korean woman leaned in. "So when Connor Forrester touches your arm, he goes *ooh*," she whispered in my ear.

My eyes flew open. This was insane. Did everyone in the entire *world* read the gossip blogs?

"Omigod, Lucy—that picture of you and Connor Forrester on the beach was just too sweet!" Maya said when we got to the trailer after lunch.

"Yeah. You snagged a good one, girlfriend," agreed Roger.

Apparently, everyone in the world *did* read the gossip blogs. "You guys! I am *not* going out with him!" I cried.

"According to this blog, you sure are," said Roger, pointing to his laptop screen.

Underneath a photo of me stuffing my face with my enchilada it read: "BREAKING NEWS: Laurel Moses's little stepsister-to-be Lisa gets her energy level up as she gets ready for another hot date with new boyfriend Connor Forrester!"

"What?! I don't even remember that being taken. I know I'm not the world's most photogenic person, but it would be nice if, once in a while, they printed a photo of me where I don't look like a total idiot." I sighed.

"Welcome to my world." Laurel sighed.

"Or got your name right," Maya added.

That, too. This was getting seriously out of control. "Can I go see if Lady A is here?" I asked. I figured if anyone could give me advice about what to do when it came to the press talking about your love life, it was her.

I found Lady A sitting on her couch wearing one of her caftans as Frederick massaged her feet. "Lucy B. Parker!" she boomed. "It's been *forever* since we've seen each other—you *must* tell me everything that's happened since then. I'm just *dying* to catch up."

That was exactly what she said the last time I saw her. It hadn't been forever; it had been two days, and obviously a lot had happened during them, which is why I was out of breath when I was done telling her all of it.

"Oh, darling—that's all just so *marvelous*!" she trilled. "I remember the blush of first love." She sighed. "Don't you, Frederick?"

He sighed, too. "I do remember, Lady A."

"Okay, (a) not only is this not FIRST love, but (b) it's not ANY love. Connor and I are just friends," I said for what felt like the thousandth time. "And the more I think about it, the more I think those little electric shocks and the fluttering in my stomach when I'm around him are because I'm allergic to him."

"Whatever you say, my dear," she said, getting off the couch and going over to the clothing rack that held her caftans. She held up an orange one. "I'd offer to let you wear one of my frocks for your first foray down the red carpet, but I fear it might be a smidge too big for you."

A smidge? I could've fit three of me in that thing.

"Plus, it would clash with the red," added Frederick.

"Uh, that's really nice, Lady A, but actually, today I got a new dress to wear. It's purple with giant flowers. And new shoes—they have cat heels," I announced proudly.

"You mean kitten heels?" asked Frederick.

"Yes, those."

"How exciting!" Lady A boomed. "You simply *must* let me do your hair and makeup! I *do* love doing other people's hair and makeup, don't I, Frederick?"

"Yes, you do, madame," he agreed.

I loved Lady A, but her makeup was more like something you'd see on a circus clown. "Actually, Laurel's hair and makeup team were—" I started to say.

"I won't take no for an answer," she interrupted, rummaging through a giant yellow toolbox.

As I saw the different tubes and palettes she took out, I got a little nervous, because they were pretty dusty, and the last thing I needed was for my face to break out because the makeup was past its expiration date. "Really—that's super-nice of you, but you totally don't have to," I said. "I'm sure you have tons of other things to do—"

"Nonsense. It'll be fun! Sadly, I never did get around to having children when I had the chance, so this can make up for it." She opened an orange toolbox and took out a bottle that said Egyptian Oil. "First, we'll start with your hair," she announced, dumping some of the oil in her hand.

Roger was going to kill me. Lady A may have been talented, but I was pretty sure she wasn't a trained professional. "I was just planning on wearing my purple flower—" I started to say.

"This stuff is just *marvelous*," she went on. "Just a touch of it gives your hair a delightful sheen that the camera just loves," she explained as she rubbed it on my hair. When she was done, she grabbed a plastic shower cap and placed it on my head. "It works better if you keep the heat in. And now we'll do your makeup," she said, dipping a small brush in one of the little pots. "But I don't want you looking until I'm done," she said, turning me away from the mirror.

"I really appreciate this," I said, "but Laurel's expecting me back—"

"Oh, darling—just shush and enjoy yourself," she ordered.

I sighed and sat back. Somehow, I had a feeling that arguing with Lady A wouldn't get me very far.

After a lot of poking and dotting and brushing, Lady A stood back to get a look at me. "Oh my, I really outdid myself this time, Frederick, didn't I?"

"You definitely did, madame," he agreed.

"It just needs one final touch," she said, rummaging in the toolbox. "Ah—here we are!" she said, holding something up that looked like spider legs.

"Are those *false eyelashes*?" I gasped.

She nodded, squeezing a tiny bit of glue out onto a brush.

"That's so cool!" I said. "I've always wanted to try those."

After she was done she stood back and gazed at me. "Much better," she said. She grabbed the shower cap off my head. "Okay, you can turn around and look at yourself now."

"Ahh!" I screamed when I got a glimpse of myself in the mirror. Not because the makeup made me look like a clown—that part I could've dealt with. I could just wash it off. But my hair was . . .

"Blue?!" I yelped. "The Egyptian Oil makes your hair *blue*?! You kind of left that part out, Lady A!"

She squinted. "Oh my. It *is* a little blue, isn't it?" she agreed. "I wonder why that is."

I picked up the bottle and looked at the label. "Maybe because the expiration date is from ten years ago?"

What was I going to do? I couldn't walk down a red carpet in a purple dress with blue hair. Talk about clashing.

I scrambled out of my seat and barely squeaked out a good-bye to Lady A and Frederick. Thank God for Roger—he'd probably yell at me for letting an untrained professional touch my hair, but at least he'd fix it for me.

Except by the time I got back to Laurel's trailer, Laurel had her nose buried in her phone and Roger and Maya were gone. Because after promising that they would do the producer's daughter's hair and makeup for her Sweet Sixteen party that weekend, they had gotten tickets to the premiere, too, and had gone back to the hotel to get ready.

Laurel looked up from texting. "Lucy, your hair is *blue*!" she cried.

"Yeah, I noticed," I said. Between this Oil Incident, the Hat Incident, and the Straightening Iron Incident, it was like all my bad luck was concentrated on my head. "What am I going to do?" I asked, starting to panic. I looked at my watch. "The screening starts in an hour."

"Okay, okay, let me think," said Laurel as she paced up and down the trailer. "You can . . . wear a hat?" she suggested.

This was just like the old days, after the Straightening Iron Incident. I had been positive that all those months of having to wear a hat because of my egghead had totally taken care of any and all bad-hair luck I may have had. I was wrong. "You can't wear a hat with a maxidress. Even I know that!" I cried. "I'll end up on OhNoYouDidNot.com for sure if I do that."

"Well, if we can make it even more blue, then you can pretend you're trying to pull a Grace Steppenwolf. You know, hair-as-fashion-statement." Grace Steppenwolf was a singer who was always dyeing her hair wacky colors like blue and pink. Once she even managed to put hearts in it for Valentine's Day. I bet her hair person had gone to lots of school for that.

I shook my head. "I can only imagine what the tab-loids would say about *that*," I moaned. Or *Mom*.

She stopped pacing. "I know—you can wear one of Lady A's turbans."

"Are you crazy?!"

"It'll look cool. And now that you're famous, you can start a trend. Like I did when I wore my sweater on inside out that time."

I remembered that. Almost every girl at my school back in Northampton ended up copying her. Even me. Except in my case I hadn't meant to do it—I had woken up late and grabbed the first thing my hand had landed on in the big pile of clothes on my floor and forgotten to look in the mirror before I ran to catch my bus.

She led me to Lady A's, who was more than happy to help us out. "What a *marvelous* idea you came up with, Laurel!" Lady A announced. I sat at her dressing room table in my new dress as she finished adjusting the gold turban that she had put on my head. "Don't you think it's a marvelous idea, Frederick?"

"I do think it's a marvelous idea, Lady A," he agreed. Except I could have sworn that I saw him shake his head a little, as in "Nope—it's totally NOT a marvelous idea!"

"You think so?" Laurel asked, pleased.

"Oh yes," she replied. "It's the perfect complement to the dress. *Very* Talitha Getty 1968, don't you think, Frederick?"

"Yes, very Talitha, Lady A," he agreed.

I didn't know who this Getty person was, but the way they were going on about it, it sounded like it was a good thing.

She stood back. "There. Now it's perfect."

I reached up to pat it. It kind of felt like I had a bird's nest on my head, but that was better than walking down a red carpet with blue hair.

I turned to Laurel. "What do you think?"

"I like it," she said. "It's very... fortune-teller-esque."

She wasn't wrong. But I liked to think that because of the gold and the dress, I looked like an *expensive* fortune-teller—not like Madame Zara, the one with the big MADAME ZARA—PCYCHIC READINGS FOR $5 sign on West Eighty-fifth Street ("I don't know if I trust a psychic who can't even spell psychic right," Beatrice always said when we walked by).

Hopefully my prediction that things could only get better was right.

chapter 14

Dear Dr. Maude,

Guess where I am RIGHT NOW?? Okay, you'll never guess, so I'll tell you. I'm in the car on the way to my very first movie premiere, and it's going to have a red carpet and everything! Laurel's agent got us invitations, and I'm super-excited even if I am wearing a turban because my hair is blue. That part is kind of a long story, so I won't go into it, but the reason I'm writing you now is that I was wondering whether you had any advice about how a person who has suddenly found herself kind-of, sort-of famous can get people to leave her alone so she can go back to being a regular person?

If you read the gossip blogs, then you already know this, but they're all writing about how I'm Connor Forrester's new girlfriend, which is completely annoying, because, like I keep telling them, I'M NOT. Not only that, but they keep calling me Lisa instead of Lucy, which is even worse. I know lots of people in the world spend a lot of time trying to become famous, but my question to you is this: how do you become UNfamous?

Looking forward to hearing from you.

yours truly,
Lucy B. Parker

P.S. Not to put any pressure on you or anything for tickets, but I'm leaving in three days.

For someone who was trying to become *un*famous, tripping on the hem of her new dress as she stepped out of a limousine didn't help things. In fact, it just made the photographers go crazy, with even more flashes going off, ruining my vision even more.

"Great," I mumbled, standing up and fixing my turban, which had somehow managed to slip off to the side. I turned to Laurel, who, because she was used to heels and fame and did not have a coordination problem, was smiling away as she posed for the photographers. "Do I look okay?" I asked.

"Yeah," she said. Then she squinted. "Except one of your false eyelashes came off."

I reached up. "So that wasn't a bug I smooshed in the limo—it was a false eyelash. Then I'll just take the other one off." Except when I yanked at it, it didn't budge. I yanked again, but all that managed to do was pull *half* of it off, so it was just hanging there like a spider.

"Lisa! Over here!" yelled one of the paps as he snapped a photo.

Great. Now there would be a picture of me looking like I had a spider hanging off my eye floating around the Internet. "I keep telling you guys—IT'S LUCY! LUCY B. PARKER!" I yelled.

"You tell 'em, dude," said a voice behind me.

I turned around to see Connor standing there. Looking very cute. Which, when you're trying to figure out if you kind-of, sort-of, maybe have a crush on someone, is NOT helpful.

"Hey," I said. I smacked my stomach in hopes of stopping the fluttering that had started.

"Well, that's a totally rad getup. You look like a gypsy. Wait—my publicist didn't tell me we were supposed to wear *costumes* to this thing," he said.

"You're not. I just— See, Lady A—" I sighed. There was no way I could explain it. "Oh, just forget it."

He squinted. "What's hanging off your eye?"

"A false eyelash," I replied. "I can't get it off. It's stuck because of the glue."

"Let me see if I can do it," he said, reaching for it.

As he yanked, another round of flashes went off. It didn't budge.

"Look at the happy couple!" someone yelled.

"OW!" I yelled as he yanked really hard.

"Here you go," he said, holding it toward me. A flash-bulb went off. I could only imagine what they'd write underneath *that* picture.

Austin tapped us on the shoulder. "You guys ready to hit it?" he asked, motioning to the red carpet.

"Wait a minute," I said nervously. "You want *me* to walk down *that* with *him*?" I squeaked, pointing at Connor.

The three of them nodded. Oh God. This was so going to look like a date. I wondered if I could sneak around to a back entrance, but when there's a chorus of "Come on—move it already! Start walking!"s behind you, and Connor's publicist Sandi is pushing you, you don't have much of a choice.

Connor put his hand out. "Ready?"

I sighed. "I guess," I replied as I took it. It was even softer and squishier than before. Did he use hand cream? Maybe I'd ask him for some beauty tips later.

Thankfully, I was able to make it down the red carpet without tripping again, or losing my turban. My eyes, however, were in bad shape from all the flashes and the False Eyelash Incident. "Connor! Lisa!" yelled the photographers.

Connor stopped walking. "It's not Lisa—it's Lucy B. Parker," he corrected them.

I turned to him and gave him a grateful smile. If I had had time to take my advice book out, I would've written, *If you're going to kind-of, sort-of, maybe have a crush on someone, make sure it's someone who realizes how impor-tant it is to you that people get your name right.*

The movie was as good as I had hoped, but I found it hard to focus because it seemed like every time I went to grab for some popcorn, Connor did, too, which meant that our hands touched. And every time that happened, it felt a little like sticking my finger in an electrical outlet, and I yanked mine back so hard that popcorn went flying—sometimes into people's hair—which was too bad because it was really good popcorn, with just the right amount of real butter on it.

"Sorry," I whispered as the woman sitting in front of me turned around and gave me a dirty look. I thought about reaching forward and picking out the piece of pop-corn that was caught in her bob, but with my luck I'd cause more of a mess, so I didn't.

I was really confused. Once we had finally sat down in the theater, and I didn't have to concentrate on walk-ing, all my nervousness had gone away and it became easy to talk to Connor. What was going on here? Why was he so nice? And funny? And not anything like I thought a big superstar would be?

It was like I was nervous that I wasn't nervous around Connor. Plus, Connor Forrester didn't like girls like me—he liked Bikini Butt blondes. I had to keep remind-ing myself of that.

I was glad when the movie was over and we walked across the street to what Laurel had explained was called the "after-party." Maybe I could manage to slip away from him so I didn't have to keep being nervous about the fact that he didn't make me nervous. It wasn't like I had anyone else to hang out with, though, seeing that Laurel and Austin were still joined at the hip. According to her, after-parties were like giant bar mitzvahs for adults, where they walked around giving each other air kisses and telling each other how great they looked to their faces, only to say mean things about one another once they walked away. It sounded a lot like what happened on *The Real Tenth Graders of New Jersey.* I was hoping there was at least really good food, but instead it was a bunch of expensive but gross stuff, like shrimp and sushi.

"Aw, man—more sushi?" said Connor when he saw it. "Why can't they just serve normal stuff like ... burgers and fries?"

My stomach grumbled. If I was trying to find reasons not to like him, that was definitely not helping.

He turned to me. "I'm starving. Want to take off?" he whispered.

"To where?"

"To a very important L.A. landmark," he replied.

A half hour later we were screaming our orders into the In-N-Out Burger's drive-through loudspeaker from the backseat of the tinted-window SUV that Connor and Austin had rented for the night, driven by a very large man named Calvin. Calvin, I learned during the ride over, used to play football in college and could have been in the pros if he hadn't hurt his knee, and now he wanted to open up a bakery based on the recipes of his grandmother from Alabama. We had asked Laurel and Austin if they wanted to come, but they were too busy making googly eyes at each other, so after we got our food, Calvin would drive me back to Shutters and then Connor back to Malibu.

Even though it was late, In-N-Out was packed, which is why we decided to eat in the car. That, and we didn't want to give the reporters any more reason to think we were a couple. We got our food, and from my first bite, I was in heaven. "You were right—this really is the best cheeseburger in the world," I said. From the fact that there were so many limos in the parking lot, you could tell that famous people liked them, too.

"And I bet you've never had animal-style fries before, huh?" he asked.

I shook my head. Animal-style meant the fries were covered with cheese, onions, and Thousand Island dressing. "Whoops," I said as part of the mixture fell on my dress. I guess you could dress a girl up and put her in a turban, but you couldn't take away her coordination issues.

He laughed. "You really are cool, Lucy B. Parker."

"Yeah, right."

"You are," he said quietly. As he bowed his head, a lock of hair flopped in his eye. I don't know why that made the fluttering speed up, but it did. "You're funny, and smart, and you eat bread—"

I felt my face turn red, and my turban slid down over my ear. "I don't know why you California people think that's so cool, but, yeah, I eat bread. And a lot of it. I also eat bagels, and knishes, and empanadas—" I babbled. Why did the oversharing thing have to start up *now*? I shoved the turban back into place.

"Most girls I know, they just talk about clothes and stuff, and they flip their hair around and bat their eyelashes and just watch you eat. And for some reason they're always, like, agreeing with me. You, though—you barely ever do."

"That's not true," I said.

He laughed. "See—you did it right there." He squinted at my ear. "Hey, is your hair blue?"

I adjusted my turban, which had slid to the side again. "Uh, yeah. It's kind of a long story, so I won't go into it now. Anyway, you were saying—"

He looked down at his fries. "It's too bad you don't live in L.A."

"Why?"

He shrugged. "I don't know. So we could … hang out. I mean, I think I kind-of, sort-of … *like* you."

My heart started beating really fast. "Like . . . like me–like me?" I asked.

He nodded. Now *he* was the one turning all red. He pointed to my eyes. "That's cool."

"What?"

"Your eyes—your pupils are really big."

Uh-oh. Last night, Laurel and I went online to get another look at the warning signs of crushes. Big pupils were number seven on the list.

He moved closer. Was he going to kiss me? Did I *want* him to kiss me? What about the fact that Calvin was in the front seat? And the fact that the burgers and fries had onions on them? And did this mean I DID have a crush on Connor? And what if I ultimately decided that Blair really was my local crush? Did kissing Connor mean that I couldn't have a crush on Blair? THIS was why I wasn't sure if I was ready for crushes—they were so confusing!

And then . . . out of the corner of my eye, I saw her.

She was walking out of the restaurant holding a white bag just like the one that was sitting on my lap and leaking grease onto my new dress, and then she got into the back of one of the limos.

Dr. Maude.

"OH MY GOD! Calvin! Follow that limo!" I yelled, pointing at Dr. Maude's car.

"Huh?" asked Calvin and Connor at the same time.

"That limo!" I yelped. "Dr. Maude is in it!"

"You mean Dr. Maude-Dr. Maude?" Calvin said. "From *Come On, People—Get with the Program*? Man, I love her," he exclaimed, starting up the car and backing out of the parking space. "And I really need to talk to her—I need some serious advice about my girlfriend."

"Okay, but I'm going first," I said. "I've been trying to track her down for months." Finally—I was *thisclose* to getting the answers I needed. Not only that, but I had avoided a kiss with Connor.

Well, I *was* thisclose to getting the answers I needed, until Calvin bashed into another car in the parking lot as it backed up at the same time he did. "Whoops," he said.

"But she's getting away!" I cried as her limo moved up to the exit and put on its blinker.

Another very tall, very big man who looked very unhappy got out of the other car and started yelling at Calvin. I jumped out of the car, not caring when the lid of my chocolate shake came off and splattered all over my dress. Calling on all the speed I had saved up by using my Please-excuse-Lucy-from-gym-class-as-she-is-menstruating note and not taking gym for the last few years, I put it all into my sprint across the parking lot.

"Dr. Maude!" I yelled at the top of my lungs, hoping she could hear me through the closed window. But I was too late. Just as I got to the exit, the limo made a right-hand turn and peeled off onto Sunset Boulevard, leaving me standing there advice-less, and covered with chocolate milk shake.

"Hey, you lost your shoe," Connor said, holding it out to me as he joined me.

I looked down. He was right—I had only one on. I hadn't even noticed. "Thanks," I said glumly, shoving my foot back into it. My turban slid down over one eye, and I shoved it back into place.

"Well, that's a bummer, huh?" he asked.

I nodded.

"What would you have asked her if you had caught up with her?"

That was a good question. I felt like I had so many problems and needed so much advice, I wouldn't have known where to start. Crushes, Ziggy, Mom, fighting with a frister. But as I looked up at Connor, who, for some reason, at *that* moment, at *that* angle, with *that* amount of moonlight shining down on him, looked even cuter than he had that night on the beach during sunset, I blurted out, "I think I would've asked her what you were supposed to do to let a boy know that you wouldn't hit him or anything like that if he tried to kiss you."

"Really?" he asked shyly.

Oh my God—what had I just done? Had I just *asked* Connor Forrester to kiss me?

"You want me to kiss you right here?" he asked

nervously. "In the middle of Sunset Boulevard? With all these cars whizzing by?"

"I never said I *wanted* you to kiss me," I said defensively, giving up on straightening my turban and just taking it off. "All I meant was that if you *tried* to kiss me, I wouldn't, you know, bash you over the head with my shoe or anything. That's a totally different thing than *wanting* someone to kiss you. Or *asking* them to."

"Oh," he said, disappointed. "So you *don't* want me to kiss you."

"Well, I didn't say that, either," I corrected. What did I want? I didn't even know. I looked over at Calvin, who was done exchanging information with the other guy and was waiting for us to get back in the car. "We should probably get going," I said, turning and walking toward the SUV.

"Hey, Lucy?" he called.

I stopped and turned around. "What?"

Just then, in front of all of the cars in the parking lot of In-N-Out—not to mention the ones on Sunset Boulevard, which, according to one of the guidebooks I had read, was one of the busiest streets in all of L.A.—Connor Forrester put his hands on my shoulders, pulled me toward him, and kissed me.

It wasn't a super-long kiss, but it was definitely a real kiss.

And the best part of it? Other than the fact that it wasn't half as scary as I thought it was going to be and it happened so fast that I didn't have a chance to be nervous?

There were no cameras around to snap a picture of it.

chapter 15

Dear Dr. Maude,

You don't know this, but I saw you the other night. At In-N-Out Burger. I guess liking burgers is another thing we have in common, besides the fact that we live in the same apartment building and we both like dogs.

I tried to catch up to you, but obviously I didn't. Which I guess worked out for the best, because if I had, I might not have had my first kiss. I know having a first kiss in the middle of the parking lot of a hamburger place isn't all that romantic, especially if you kind-of, sort-of ask the person to kiss you instead of letting it just happen naturally, but whatever. It was with Connor Forrester, if you can believe that. It's okay if you can't, because I still can't, and I was there when it happened! (It's not listed as one of "50 Fun Facts about Connor" on his website, but he happens to have very soft lips.)

Beatrice and Alice and Marissa are totally going to freak out when they hear about it. I haven't even told Laurel yet, if you can believe it. Partly because I've wanted to keep it to myself for a bit, and partly because I don't want to hurt her feelings on account of the fact that she and Austin never ended up having an offscreen kiss because there were always photographers around. Which means that I officially had my first real kiss before she did. And she's older! And famous!

To be honest, I don't know how I feel about the whole kissing thing. It was kind of interesting, but I'm not so sure I want to do it on a regular basis yet. Luckily, Connor doesn't have braces, so my lip didn't get cut up, but it WAS a little slimy. We hung out a few times afterward (I finally got to go on the Haunted Hollywood tour!), but because of the distance and stuff, we're not going to be boyfriend/girlfriend. Which is good, because I still don't know how I feel about this crushing thing. We are, however, now Facebook friends. Who knows—maybe if Blair and I get to know each other better, I really WILL develop a crush on him (after hanging out with Connor, I'm now pretty certain that I did not have a real crush on Blair) and will want to kiss him at some point. But maybe not.

Anyway, hopefully I'll run into you when we're both back in New York. Because even though Laurel and I have been getting along a lot better, and Mom e-mailed me yesterday to say that their trip is going really well, and she misses me, and in a few weeks we're going to go to Cape Cod for the weekend, just her and me (we better not stop at any bra stores on the drive up!), if things continue to be as crazy as they've been, I'm still going to be needing LOTS of advice.

yours truly,

S.W.A.K.

(That stands for "Sealed with a Kiss," in case you didn't know.)

LUCY B. PARKER

Even if you feel bad for a person because, although she's older, you got kissed before she did, there's only so long you can keep that news a complete secret. Which is why, as we were flying over Iowa on our way back to New York (because Lady A was still having trouble remembering her lines, the movie was behind schedule, which meant that Laurel got enough time off to come back to New York for a few days), I turned to Laurel and said, "There's something I need to talk to you about."

"Oh no. Are you mad at me?" she asked anxiously. "Have I been doing the superstar thing again? I made sure to tell Marci *not* to tip off the press this time. Didn't you see how there were a lot less paps at the airport?"

"No, no—I'm not mad at you at all," I replied. "In fact, I'm a little afraid that after what I'm about to tell you, you might be mad at *me*."

"You finally decided to shave your legs and you used my razor and now the blade is all dull?"

"What? No!" I said. As much as I really didn't want

to shave my legs, now that it was officially summer and therefore shorts weather, I was thinking I probably should so that I didn't scare any small children I might come across in Central Park. Plus my hair had recovered from the Egyptian oil mess, and I didn't want to tempt fate. I took a deep breath. "I . . . kissed Connor."

"You kissed Connor Forrester?!" she yelled. "When?"

"Shhhh," I whispered as the rest of the people in first class turned around to look at me. Luckily, they were all pretty old, because flying first class costs a lot of money, and so I hoped they didn't know who he was. But still, it was embarrassing. "In the parking lot of In-N-Out Burger. After the premiere the other night."

"You had your first kiss in a parking lot?!" Laurel yelled.

I clamped my hand down on her mouth. "Laurel! If you don't stop doing that, I'm not going to tell you the story!"

She removed my hand. "Okay, okay," she whispered. "I'm sorry. Now tell me everything."

I did. And as I did, I felt a huge sense of relief, kind of like when you've been in the car for a long time and you really have to pee and you finally get to a rest stop.

When I was done, she wrinkled her nose. "It was slimy? Really?"

I shrugged. "Yeah, kind of. So maybe the fact that you didn't get to kiss Austin isn't such a bad thing!" I said brightly. Frankly, I was pretty surprised that someone who got as freaked out about germs as Laurel did would even consider kissing someone in the first place. "So are you mad at me?"

"Do you mean because if the tables were turned, I totally would've told you right away instead of keeping it a secret for three whole days?" she asked.

"No. I mean because you're older and I kissed someone before you did."

Her face fell. "Oh. Well, I hadn't really thought about it, but now that you put it that way—"

Oh great. Now she *was* going to be mad at me.

"—no. Not really," she went on. "I mean, I've kind of gotten used to the fact that there's a lot of stuff I may have done before you—like, you know, going to awards shows, and flying on private jets. But in terms of regular stuff—like going to the mall, and sleepovers, and kissing—you're sort of ahead of me on that front."

"And getting yelled at for having a messy room," I added. "I'm ahead of you with that, too."

She laughed. "Yeah, with that one, I don't think you have to worry. But seriously—I'm happy for you. And before you even say it, I'll say it for you: I promise I won't tell anyone. I swear on Miss Piggy's life."

I smiled. "Thanks," I said.

That's what happened when you were BFFs with someone: they could read your mind.

When we got off the plane in New York, Mom and Alan were waiting for us. It was nice to see them all tan and rested, but I could've done without seeing the big goofy smiles on their faces on account of the fact that Marissa had once told me that goofy smiles were a side effect of doing it a lot, and I did NOT want to think about them in that way.

As we were driving into the city from Queens, which is where JFK was, a really cool thing happened—like suddenly everything looked familiar. And when I got out of the car, Pete gave me a ginormous hug. And when I went to the bodega to get a soda, Mr. Kim, who owned it, said, "Long time, no see, Lucy B." And when I waved to Gurpreet, who owned the newsstand, he waved back.

For the first time in two months after leaving Northampton, I felt like I was . . . *home*. And not just home in terms of where all my stuff was, but home-home. Totally content and comfortable. As if I had just finished eating a sundae with the perfect ratio of hot caramel to ice cream while wearing my softest pair of pajamas.

"So you had fun?" Mom asked later as she helped me unpack. For her, that meant putting things that hadn't been worn back into their proper places—for me, it meant just trying to throw everything in the closet without her seeing and dealing with it later.

"Uh-huh," I said.

"You and Laurel got along well?" she asked.

I nodded. I decided going into the whole story of Laurel being a jerk and then our make-up fight was a waste of time, because the truth was, we worked through stuff and it was okay now. And Mom would just go tell Alan, who would freak out all over again. Not that Laurel and I wouldn't fight again, because we probably would. But that was okay, too, because it meant we were fristers and we loved each other.

She flopped down next to me on the bed. "So what was your favorite part of the trip?

What *was* my favorite part? Ordering pancakes for dinner from room service? Walking-slash-tripping down the red carpet? Lady A giving me her *personal* e-mail address so we could keep in touch? Finding out what it felt like to have a crush? Being kissed for the very first time? Laurel telling me I was her best friend?

"I'm not sure yet," I said. "Kind of a lot happened. It's a long story."

"Come on, Lucy. I want to hear everything!" Mom said.

I smiled. It was nice having my mom back. "Okay," I said, flopping down next to her.

Although maybe I'd leave the kiss part out for now.

chapter 16

Dear Dr. Maude,

I've been home for a few days now, and I think I'm finally over my jet lag. And you want to know the coolest thing? For the first time, it really DOES feel like home. Just like it's starting to feel like Laurel and I really ARE sisters.

I keep waiting for something huge to happen now that I've been kissed. Like, maybe, my period to arrive. But it still hasn't. Although Marissa just sent me an e-mail saying that she overheard a girl at the Northampton community pool say that if you drink ginger tea and stand on your head for fifteen minutes a day, that should do the trick. Would you happen to know if that's true? Or where I can find ginger tea in our neighborhood?

Anyway, I have to go, because Laurel and I are going to the movies to see Austin and Connor's new movie *Apin'—American Style*. Have you heard about it? It's about a chimp that comes to live with an American family as part of a foreign exchange program. It's supposed to be really good.

If you want to hang out one day, let me know. Laurel has to go back to L.A. for the movie, and all of my friends (all two of them) are at camp, so I'm around. And I have a feeling I'm going to need a break from all the quality-time activities that Mom has planned for us.

yours truly,
LUCY B. PARKER

An Interview with Robin Palmer, by Lucy B. Parker

Q: As you know, I'm in middle school. I know you're a lot older than me, but do you remember what you were like back then? Did you have as many embarrassing moments as me?

A: You're right—middle school was a long time ago for me. But I still remember it like it was yesterday. I was actually a lot like you, Lucy. You know how you want to get your period and hate wearing a bra? Well, I felt the same way... and, unfortunately, I needed a bra really early, which was completely embarrassing and had me crossing my arms in front of my chest a lot.

When I think of middle school, I remember reading Judy Blume books in my room with a flashlight when I was supposed to be sleeping. I would read her books and feel this huge sense of relief. She just totally, completely understood me. It made me feel like I wasn't the only one having a tough time. And now when I'm lucky enough to get e-mails from readers who say that I do the same thing for them, it's the biggest honor in the world, because I know how much it means at that age to feel like someone just gets you.

As for embarrassing moments, I'm sure I did have as many as you, but because I'm so old I conveniently can't remember them.

Q: You weren't always a writer, though, were you? Didn't you live in L.A.? I hope this won't be considered bloversharing, but I don't really like it out there. Mainly because no one eats bread.

A: You're right—barely anyone does eat bread there, which I think is part of the reason I moved to New York. And

I wasn't always a writer. I always wanted to be one, but I was too afraid to show people stuff I had written. I thought you had to be a really special kind of person to write, but now I know you just have to sit down and do it. So after I graduated from college, I moved out to Hollywood and worked in the television business. It was a lot of fun, and I got to meet some famous people and to go on the sets of some movies and premieres, but at my thirtieth birthday party, I remembered how I felt when, in second grade, Mrs. Rokosny had read a story I had written to the class. It was the most incredible feeling in the world. So I left my job and started writing. And writing. And writing. And writing. And then I wrote a book for teens called *Cindy Ella*, and the rest is history!

Q: As you know, I keep two logs—one that lists when all the girls in my grade got their periods, and the other that lists their three crushes. Did you keep logs when you were a kid?

A: Sadly, I was not smart enough at your age to come up with such a genius idea. But you and I are alike in a lot of other ways. For instance, we both think Billy's Bakery has the best cupcakes in New York City. And we both love cats. (Although my two—Onyx and O'Neill—are a little nicer to me than Miss Piggy is to you.) And we both like to wear a lot of color. And my first friend when I moved to New York was my doorman, who was, strangely enough, also named Pete. And I have a lot of experience knowing what it's like to be the New Girl in school, too, because I moved a bunch of times. I did not, however, send e-mails to anyone who was like Dr. Maude, because back in the old days we didn't have e-mail! Okay, Lucy, we have to stop talking about this because it's making me feel very old.

When I'm not busy overlistening to my mom's conversations or keeping the Official Crush Log of the Center for Creative Learning, I'm updating my Web site!

LUCYBPARKER.com

Check out my site for:

- A sneak peek at upcoming books

- My personal "Why Me?" diary

- The purr-fectly funny "As Seen by Miss Piggy" feature

- Author Robin Palmer's advice column (She's a LOT better at responding than Dr. Maude!)

- Fun downloadables and more exclusive content!

Get to know Lucy B.!

yours truly,
LUCY B. PARKER 1:
girl vs. superstar

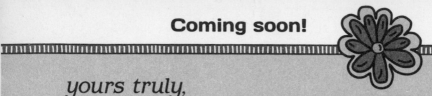